TEAR-LACED EYES

When Keino slid into bed next to her it was like placing kindling on a blazing fire. They were consumed by one another. Their bodies were so intertwined, touching and tasting, there were times when they felt as if they had melted together.

Keino repeated Amara's name as though it were a chant as he suckled, stroked, and caressed her.

Amara was engulfed by the electricity of his touch, the erratic rhythm of her heart and the heat that was enveloping her, and then he began to enter her with all the finesse of a master.

As she flinched and became still in his arms he was struck by his inability to move any farther. He stopped, held Amara close while he looked in her now tear-laced eyes.

A FOREIGN AFFAIR

Chilufiya Safaa

KENSINGTON PUBLISHING CORP.
http://www.kensingtonbooks.com

DAFINA BOOKS are published by

Kensington Publishing Corp.
850 Third Avenue
New York, NY 10022

All Kensington titles, imprints and distributed lines are
available at special quantity discounts for bulk purchases
for sales promotion, premiums, fund-raising, educational
or institutional use.

Special book excerpts or customized printings can also
be created to fit specific needs. For details, write or phone
the office of the Kensington Special Sales Manager: Kensington Publishing Corp., 850 Third Avenue, New York,
NY 10022. Attn. Special Sales Department. Phone:
1-800-221-2647.

Dafina and the Dafina logo Reg. U.S. Pat. & TM Off.

First Printing: June 2005
10 9 8 7 6 5 4 3 2 1

Printed in the United States of America

To my children and my grandchildren:
You are the light in my life—
you give my life meaning
All my love,
Mom / Nana / Grammy

ACKNOWLEDGMENTS

Thanks to my Creator for flights of
fancy and fantasy.

To Lisa Johnson for tireless typing of the manuscript.

To Ms. Vivian Stephens, founder of RWA, mentor extraordinaire—your wisdom and wealth of information have been invaluable.

My Wee Li'l People family—I love you all (that includes you, Erika).

DiDi, thanks for helping to keep the crown straight.

Rochelle Alers for your generosity and encouragement—I'll never forget.

Karen Thomas and Nicole Bruce—your energy in bringing *A Foreign Affair* to print will always be appreciated.

Friends J. Buist, J. Shaffer and J. Wilson, who kept saying "Chilufiya, you can do it!" You were right. Thank you.

Simone and Barbara—you saw the book before I wrote it. Thank you.

For all of the energy sent my way through prayers and good thoughts—many thanks.

Michael, Judy, Lauren and Jason—the first prototype will always be my favorite!

Chapter 1

NAIROBI, KENYA

At three A.M., Keino Mazrui stood in mahogany magnificence, with taut glistening skin poured over a perfectly toned mass of sinewy flesh, looking out at the black velvet Kenyan sky. His exquisite, classically African face masterfully chiseled, with flaring nostrils and piercing obsidian eyes, was wrapped in pensive reflection as the darkness enveloped him. He stood contemplating his future. He had been born in Nairobi, Kenya, thirty-five years ago. He proudly wore the mantle of the eldest son of His Honor Judge Garsen Mazrui, a Kenyan whose lineage was Kikuyu, and the beautiful Adina Mazrui, an Ethiopian of Amharic descent. Keino's ancestry alone made him an extraordinary individual, for after all, he was the product of two extremely intelligent people who had at a time when it was rarely done, in the African world, defied convention by marrying one another, and they had triumphed.

Being the progeny of a wealthy and powerful family had afforded Keino and his three brothers lives of privilege, leisure, and in keeping with continental African tradition, immense responsibility. Keino felt tied to so many traditions and edicts. Often as he journeyed through his life, he felt it was not his own, but that he lived for ancestral conventions and precepts long ago forged by people of whom he had only heard. One of the unwritten statutes was that family was everything, past, present and future. Even during his college years, while he was being educated in the most prestigious institutions Europe and America had to offer, he knew this would not change. Even his pursuit of law and business degrees was in line not only with his sensibilities and talents but with the family vision for his future.

Keino stood in the bleakness of night pondering his plight, for he knew that the obligations of being born first in a prominent Kenyan family continued to exist regardless of Western acculturation.

Yes, his life had been an extraordinary one—well educated, well traveled—a very productive life. Even as he practiced in the law firm his father founded he still managed to create a very lucrative international trading business, which was growing rapidly.

Yet, here he was, facing his greatest challenge. How much of his life did he owe to ancestral canon? Was he really bound by familial law to reach into the future by making the ultimate connection in the present?

Keino had known women, few in the biblical sense for he was too private a soul to take lightly what was to him considered sacred. Though he had met women the world over none had touched his spirit. He too had been waiting! He could not live through a marriage of convenience, an arranged covenant. Yet he knew that if he could not find that soul who made his spirit dance, his father would surely take matters into his own hands and for the good of family he would acquiesce.

His father's pronouncement at dinner had caught him off guard, even though it was not totally unexpected. His Honor Judge Garsen Mazrui had made it clear that his eldest son, Keino, had one year left to be without a wife and an heir. Judge Mazrui was a man whose pronouncements were never to be taken lightly. His Honor was as powerful in his world as he was in his home. He seldom heard the word "No," and when he did he was always certain he had heard incorrectly. The law firm that he established before becoming a judge was the most influential firm in Nairobi. He had been on the bench for the past thirty years. His connections were global, for he, like his sons after him, had been educated in Europe and America for university studies. Garsen Mazrui was well thought of in all of the circles in which he traveled. He was seen as a man of intelligence, integrity and prodigious ingenuity.

As a middle-aged man his looks were striking. His son Keino had inherited his chiseled bone structure, however, where Keino's face was softened by his mother's genetic code, his father's face was all lines and angles. His jaw, which was always seemingly set for battle, was adorned by a beard peppered with silver to match that which appeared near both temples. Already a tall man, standing well over six feet, the judge's erect posture, and rich baritone when speaking, made him appear to be an imposing figure. Laughter, on the rare occasions when it was expressed, was shared mostly with his adored wife and family. For his power and accomplishments he thanked his God, but his wife and family were what he lived for and they alone knew that there was a private vulnerability that ran through the core of the great judge.

He did not relish reminding his children of their responsibilities, particularly Keino, for Keino had a will of iron, but Keino's wife had been chosen when he was but a child. She was now a fully-grown, beautiful, well-educated Kenyan woman and she was waiting. Keino knew the rules. He had had ample time to make another decision and release everyone from the agreement but he had not done so. The two families whose social and financial affairs had been linked for generations were waiting.

Because Judge Mazrui's own marriage had been an unconventional one, he had wished his sons not to have the struggles one faced going against conventional wisdom. His three younger sons had complied and they were doing well and their wives and children were blessed family additions. Keino was another story. Always one to march to his own music down his own path, this ultimatum might prove difficult. Dear God, why couldn't Keino just follow the rules? As the question rushed to his mind to be answered, Judge Mazrui had to laugh aloud to himself as the answer came swiftly and clearly. *He is your son and tradition didn't stop you from possessing your beautiful Adina.*

"So it didn't," he said softly to himself. "We shall see where Keino's path takes him."

The heavy darkness of the night had crept along at a snail's pace. Keino had been unable to allow the comfort of slumber to overtake him. He felt as though his life had taken a turn to which he was not privy.

As the dawn moved over the horizon Keino knew there was one place where he could find solace. Sorting through conflicting thoughts and endless streams of contradictions was work for the matriarch of his family. His mother, Adina. His mother was a spectacular woman. It was easy to see why his Kenyan father had broken tradition and wed his majestic mother, an Ethiopian woman. Regal was the only way to describe Keino's mother. Nobility for sure, but with a quiet charm and warmth that drew people to her. Her oval face, a rich cinnamon gold, always carried a ready smile on full lips. Her eyes were her most beguiling feature because her smiles were always captured there. A very content woman, Adina Mazrui wore her beauty, her intelligence and her satisfaction with her life all with equal comfort.

Keino's parents had met at college. Their souls had known one another instantly he had always been told. From the looks he saw pass between them when they were together he was sure the story was true. When his mother looked at his father it was clear that she saw in him all of the security she would ever need, and when he looked at her he saw all of the beauty he could ever behold and he proclaimed that often to anyone who would listen.

As Keino thought of the two of them a distant smile spread across his ruggedly handsome face. Yes, he was home. Though he had recently moved to Virginia for purposes of expanding an escalating business, it was here to Kenya where he came to renew his soul, to rejuvenate his spirit. Kenya, the cradle of civilization, had indeed rocked and nurtured him. He looked forward to one day returning permanently to the land of his birth and that of his paternal ancestors.

Now, he rose slowly, his movements never wasted, his regal bearing in place as he prepared to shower and ready himself for the day. As he descended the stairs of his parents' palatial home a calm embraced him as he remembered many happy hours spent in this grand place. The grandeur did not, however, diminish the warmth and comfort it exuded. The day was already sunny and beautiful. The air was tinged with a comforting breeze.

As he continued walking he could hear the laughter of children. He knew those sounds. They were the sounds of the children of his brothers. His nieces and nephews, three of each. They were the delight of their grandparents' lives. He entered the beautifully appointed dining room to shouts of, "Uncle Keino is here," with children popping up from everywhere, dressed casually in Western clothing, offering kisses and hugs. Lots of love was one of the trademarks of the Mazrui family. His mother sat smiling in a room signified by opulence, refinement and meticulous attention to detail. She was the first to speak as she arose from one of the matching eighteenth century chairs which graced the dining table. With arms reaching for her eldest son she said in loving tones to the children, "Please, my darlings, let Uncle Keino come in and sit down"—smiling all the while at the mob scene that was her six grandchildren. She was so proud of her sons, the women they had married and the beautiful children who completed their families.

Today was the first Saturday of the month. The first Saturday was Adina Mazrui's day to have a two-hour breakfast conversation with her grands to catch up on their lives and to pass along to them pieces of the family history she felt it was important that they remember.

Keino approached his mother with clear admiration in his eyes. "I see you are still doting on this brood of yours in your ritualistic way."

"Yes, I am," his mother answered as they embraced, "and I am enjoying every moment of it."

As Adina spoke, Mrs. Dula, a family cook, entered the room with trays of traditional Kenyan and Ethiopian dishes mixed with some of the children's Western favorites. A veritable feast, pancakes, waffles, omelets, sweet porridge fritters made with dark brown sugar, avocado and papaya salad, minced lamb kebabs, kitifo leb leb—an Ethiopian version of steak tartare—spice tea and various juices completed the meal. The children chattered on, delighting their grandmother and uncle with stories of school and various social activities. Keino sat wondering what it would be like to have his own progeny as a part of this gathering. His mother observed him as he interacted with the children and she could almost read his mind, for his thoughts were not far from hers.

Soon the children slowly excused themselves from the table one by one, saying good-byes to their grandmother and uncle with physical and verbal demonstrations of affection. A driver waited to transport them to their respective homes.

After the departure of the last child, Keino put his arm around his mother and led her into her sitting room. This room, like his mother, had endured the ravages of time and become even more impressive. Elegance and comfort lived here side by side amid a hand-carved Italian Renaissance desk, lush folds of silk and brocade, intricately carved chairs with softly clawed feet and plush Turkoman rugs were enhanced by sprinkles of traditional and contemporary African art collected from years of travel and appreciation.

This room had been the confidante to so many family conversations. Today was Keino's turn. His mother spoke: "Keino, my darling son, it has been so wonderful having you home for these past few days. Though you have traveled away from home much of your adult life, these years I am missing you more than ever. I suppose I will never tire of dreaming of the day when all of my sons, their wives and children are close to me. You know that family is everything to me.

"Enough about my wishes and dreams. How are you, my son?"

Keino loved his mother with all of his heart and with that realization looked into her face and said, "Mother, I am fine, a bit weary from travel but work is exhilarating. Watching my creation take hold has been quite a boost to my life."

"Your father and I are so very proud of you, you know, my darling," she said with a smile.

"We could sit here all day and talk about business, but as your mother I can also discern when something is troubling you. I think I know, but would you like to share your thoughts with a mom who worries too much?"

"At this moment, Mother, you are perhaps the only one with whom I can share these thoughts. I am concerned about Dad's ultimatum last night. Though I want what he wants I am not sure I can oblige him this year. Asking for more time is out of the question. I have already gotten a five-year reprieve," he said with a hint of humor in his voice. "Had the business not been moving at breakneck speed it is doubtful that I would have been given as much time. I am looking for a way to make peace with my fate. I am my father's son; I take seriously my obligations and responsibilities, but perhaps I spent too much time in the West. I am looking for more. I know the difficulties you and father faced when you broke with tradition to marry one another, but I am willing to risk disapproval and disappointment rather than marry a woman for whom my soul does not burn. I need to look at my woman as father looks at you. I need her to be my confidante, my port in storms. I need what I've grown up seeing. My three brothers found it. I need to find it. I have traveled the world but, Mother, I have not seen her and I know that the bride chosen at my birth is not the one. Makena is lovely, she is intelligent and she was groomed for me, but she is not the one."

Adina Mazrui saw the despair in her son's eyes and willed herself a way to comfort him. "Keino," she said, "you were my firstborn—precocious, willful, always your own person. You are today a powerful man, greatness surrounds you. Seek the counsel of your Creator, my son, and when peace comes to your soul your wife will come into your life."

With that said, Adina wrapped her son in her arms as she had when he was a child and whispered, "Your father is on your side. In the end he will always come to your assistance no matter what he says to the contrary."

Keino felt comforted and knew that soon he would find the peace that he sought.

With one final embrace, he rose to prepare to return to the United States. Business was calling and to answer would be a welcome distraction.

Chapter 2

Here she was again, tossing and turning with sleep eluding her like bubbles attempting to be captured in the hands of a child. This unwelcome pattern of elusive sleep had become a consistent one over the last week. With the advent of her consulting firm, Terrell and Associates, winning the coveted Mazrui Industries account, much to her amazement, she, Amara Terrell, had been uncharacteristically nervous and edgy.

Anyone aware of her uneasiness and distress at the prospect of this new venture certainly would have questioned her sanity. She was accomplished, at the top of her class at Spelman and Harvard Business, and she was beautiful by any standard. Golden honeyed skin encased her long lean ballerina limbs, and shoulder length, silky, jet black hair framed an exquisitely crafted heart-shaped face. Most perplexing was the fact that she was losing sleep over executing a task she had performed in similar circumstances hundreds of times before. Painfully aware of this all-too-often occurrence of no sleep, Amara decided that tonight she would capture once and for all the slumber that had heretofore escaped her.

Her favorite room in her newly purchased home was her bedroom. She had gone to great lengths to make it her sanctuary. With the help of her sister Cassandra, who was an interior designer, she had decorated her entire house beautifully, but her bedroom was her pride and joy. There, she was surrounded by many of the things she loved in life. Peach colored walls to bring light to the room and calm to the soul. The crown molding in the ceiling was painted cream as was all of the other woodwork. An elaborate ecru ceiling fan hung over her four-poster canopy bed. She had chosen this bed because it symbolized for her an island of calm, a home port, an escape from reality. This beautifully handcrafted, antique, cherry wood bed, elegantly crowned with pineapple finials, was her dream bed. Tonight she hoped it would inspire pleasant dreams once again. She looked around the room deciding which ritual she'd use tonight to court the magical potion called sleep. One wall in the room had been customized to hold floor to ceiling cherry wood bookshelves complete with a gliding library ladder so that as she slept at night she would be surrounded by many of the magical words which had given her comfort during her waking hours. On the opposite wall was an étagère which housed a state-of-the-art Bose sound system and a television. To complete the picture were a cherry wood highboy, a cheval mirror, a cream colored chaise lounge with peach and apricot throws and a round table just large enough for two. The table was covered with a peach silk tablecloth hosting two Louis XIV chairs covered in the same cream color silk as the chaise lounge.

Amara decided to retire to the master bath, soak in a tub full of her favorite fragrance, put on a pair of silk pajamas, a Pachelbel CD and go to sleep. She prayed it would happen that easily. She was at a loss to determine the reason for the lack of sleep. It was, after all, a coup to have gotten the contract; it was a marvelous assignment with tremendous benefits to her small firm. Perhaps that was the problem. She had garnered comparable contracts before but not many companies really compared to Mazrui Industries. If she traced her jitters they started when her research unearthed the fact that Mr. Keino Mazrui, CEO of Mazrui Industries, was no easy taskmaster and that he had personally intervened to permanently displace the last two consulting firms hired to do exactly what she said her people could do, and he would, she was told, on occasion directly oversee her work.

Her attempts to calm herself had been unsuccessful and so she had made a mantra of repeating to herself that she was not afraid of hard work, quite the contrary, she thrived on it, but even as she attempted to still her soul a small voice reminded her that Keino Mazrui might well be a challenge beyond the norm. The prospect of meeting this man with his extensive holdings, steel trap brilliance and transcontinental jetsetting had her just a bit uneasy and for Amara, having a case of nerves about business was a new experience.

As the bright Virginia sun shone beautifully on a chilly autumn day, Amara awoke a bit more refreshed and looking forward to a gabfest with her three sisters. She had requested that they all gather in what they called their sister circle so that she could get some feedback about this highly unusual case of insomnia. She showered, dressed and prepared for the short drive to her sister Adana. Amara always enjoyed the drive to her older sister's home. It was in a more established section of Arlington, thirty minutes from the newer development in which she lived. The drive was breathtaking. Tall stately oak trees lined the roadway and all of the dwellings along the path were built as though they were designed to commune with the natural settings in which they were placed. She slipped a Floetry CD into the deck and easily maneuvered her champagne colored BMW in the direction of Adana's home.

Adana, an attorney, had been a partner in an up-and-coming law firm for a few years now and had her sights set on a judgeship. As Amara thought of her three sisters, she could only smile. These were the women who knew her best in the world, aside from their mother.

Their parents, James and Ana Terrell, had been sixties activists and had graced all four of their daughters with middle names from the continent they revered—Africa. Amara, Afiya, and Adana were the three who had chosen to use their African names instead of their American monikers. Amara's sisters were always her pride and joy. Alexandra Adana was the eldest and the most statuesque of the sisters. At five feet nine inches she was a beauty with a fashionably short haircut and slanted piercing eyes, always the attorney in and out of the courtroom.

Amber Afiya was the second daughter. Long and

graceful, a gallery owner specializing in African and African-American art from around the Diaspora, she was delicate in every way, soft-spoken and fluid of movement.

Afiya's generally braided hair was worn most often piled atop her head, wrapped in fabrics matching the flowing African or East Indian garments she preferred.

Cassandra Anika, the third daughter, an interior designer, and an avid people person, was always the flamboyant, chic one dressed to the nines, with blond highlighted shoulder length hair. Cassandra was considered a very astute business woman whose clients numbered among Virginia's most affluent.

Amara's smile was still illuminating her face as she rounded the corner and eased into the driveway of her sister's impressive colonial-style home. Cassandra's two-seater Mercedes and Afiya's late model Saab, were already parked.

Amara pulled in behind the Saab, stepped from her car, and sprinted up the paved walkway and turned her key in the lock. All of the sisters shared keys to one another's homes. They were tightly knit in many ways.

As she walked across the black and white tiled foyer she could hear conversation and laughter in the great room just beyond the entrance. So like her sisters, whether in a heated debate or just a heartfelt communion, there was always a shared love and respect.

"Amara, is that you?" She heard Adana say.

"Come on in, girl, we're waitin' for you."

"Hey, everybody," Amara said as she entered a room of smiling faces. Afiya was stretched out by the hearth of a roaring fire wearing a mud cloth caftan with burnished gold tones woven into the fabric. Today her braids hung freely. Cassandra, dressed for a later scheduled interior design appointment, sat on her sister's hunter green sofa surrounded by an array of designer accent pillows in jewel tones. She was dressed in a winter white, long sleeved sheath with matching ankle length duster trimmed in beige leather complete with beige leather, knee high boots. Adana was dressed for a previously scheduled working lunch, in a black wool pantsuit, black silk blouse, a string of pearls and matching pearl earrings. She was seated in a plush barrel chair which matched her sofa. Amara was in the most comfortable wear for Saturday chores: a peach jogging suit with matching shell and walking shoes. Amara came in and plopped down in the center of the earth-tone carpet, which covered the floor.

"What's all this laughing about?" Amara asked as she stretched her long legs in front of her. "I'll bet people can hear you in the next block," she said as she joined the contagious stream of humor.

Cassandra answered, "We were laughing at a potential client of mine who wanted me to fly to Australia to decorate a home he has built which is a cave burrowed under the ground. I told him I did not wish to go into the bowels of hell to ply my trade and he had·the nerve to be insulted."

Once again, the room erupted in laughter.

"Cassandra, you are too much," Amara said, wiping tears from her eyes.

"Now we know why Dad used to call her his little devil," quipped Afiya.

"OK, sisters, let's get serious. You know we could laugh all day," Adana began. "Let's hear from Amara;

she got us up and about on this beautiful Saturday morning—on very short notice, I might add. She must know we love her—you do, don't you, baby sis?"

Amara smiled and a thoughtful curve touched her lips as she answered, "Your love is one thing of which I am always sure. Thanks. I really need your insightfulness this morning. I am for the first time in my career feeling an uneasiness I have never experienced. I can't ever recall second-guessing myself in this way. After too many nights of troubled soul-searching my head has been reeling with self-doubt. I'm trying to find the levelheaded, in-charge, confident Amara I used to be," she said with a hint of nervous laughter. "She seems to be momentarily concealing herself. I feel wonderful about the work. I beat out some very stiff competition to get this contract, so I know my presentation was really tight. I also know that the things I presented were a true reflection of my skills and my company's capabilities. I should have nothing to worry about. What is going on with me?" she asked, desperate for an answer.

Delicate Afiya, languid almost in her approach to life, asked with a deep-set stare coming from eyes the color of black pearls, "When exactly, Amara, did all of this uneasiness begin for you?"

"Well," Amara began, "I really am not sure I can pinpoint it logically. What I come up with sounds so ridiculous."

"Try," Afiya urged.

A glazed look of despair entered Amara's eyes as she said, "Well, really, I've narrowed it down to when I discovered the proclivity of the CEO, Keino Mazrui, to fire first and ask questions later."

Cassandra, in her own flamboyant style, yelled, "I like that name—some magic in there, girl. What does he look like?"

"Cassandra, I have never seen him. There are clips and photos available, I am sure, but limited time just hasn't permitted researching his physical attributes," Amara said with a smile.

Adana, in courtroom style, interjected her thoughts. "Amara, you have already proven on more than one occasion that you and your staff are among the best in the country at what you do. Are you really going to destroy your good health by stressing yourself out over the possibility of the demise of a training contract? Not the certainty, but the possibility—Amara, how logical are you being? If we operated on the possibility of failure none of us would ever move forward."

Amara lowered her voice and spoke in exasperated tones. "I said it wasn't logical; I just get this feeling of dread and a serious case of nerves whenever I hear the name Keino Mazrui."

Afiya, the mystical one, leaned back in her chair and very quietly and slowly asked, "Have you ever considered that the ancestors are trying to tell you something, and that the something has to do with Keino Mazrui and that it doesn't have to be disaster that you are being forewarned about?"

Adana, in her style, yelled, "Afiya, now is not the time for your psychic premonitions! Everything is not spirit world, extraterrestrial, or shaman induced."

"Okay, Adana," Afiya responded. "Take your logical jurisprudence-tainted thinking and you tell us what Amara's block is. Go ahead, sweetie," she said, dripping with sarcasm, "student of Western linear thinking. Where does the straight line lead us today?"

Cassandra, barely able to contain her laughter while glancing at Amara, who was also smiling, interrupted. "All right, you two, as usual, the answer is probably somewhere in the middle.

"Amara, you know we were all taught to trust spirit, and I certainly do, so all I can say is trust that spirit is leading you to a wonderful experience and you will be prepared for wherever you are led."

Amara looked around the room and felt a deep sense of satisfaction as she studied the supportive faces of her sisters. "Thanks everyone," said Amara. "I know this was really short notice, but before Monday I had to hear some voices other than those in my head. Even though no real conclusions were drawn, I feel better. I realize also that I really do need to remember to trust spirit. Thanks again."

Hurriedly, Adana, in attorney mode, sprang to her feet. "I've got to run! I put some goodies in the kitchen for you. You all know my code. Lock up for me, will you? I'll see you at Mom and Dad's for dinner Sunday—see ya!"

"That girl truly needs to breathe," Afiya said as the blur that was Adana whirled out of the door. The other sisters laughed as they filled their plates with delectable treats.

Chapter 3

The big day arrived. It eased in like slow-moving fog perched over majestic mountaintops.

Amara's jitters had lessened. The pure professional, the founder and CEO of Terrell and Associates consulting firm took over. She mentally prepared herself to be the best professional development consultant she could be. Her staff of ten had been prepped, and she was ready to finish the preliminary assessment process with Mazrui Industries top management personnel.

Mrs. Mary Rogers, Keino Mazrui's personal assistant, had arranged a meeting at the Arlington, Virginia site. Amara would meet with thirty high level managers to get a feel for their concerns and areas of difficulty to more effectively design training manuals that could be used after her company's departure. This was the trial run. If it worked well she was guaranteed work at other Mazrui complexes in London, New York, and Nairobi, Kenya. It really was too much to think about now. *Focus on today* she reminded herself. *Focus on today.*

Amara had difficulty deciding what to wear. She was known in her circle as a high fashion dramatic dresser, a serious clothes horse. She always managed a very striking, head turning look. Her jewelry in particular made a statement. She wore bold pieces, large geometric shapes in shiny metals or one-of-a-kind wearable art objects. For the corporate world the look was toned down, but no less beautiful. Today she wanted to make sure that her competence was not questioned and that her flair for the dramatic and creative were established more in her boardroom presentations than from the racks in her closets. She settled for a black and white, bold-checked houndstooth de la Renta suit with a mandarin collar and a slim skirt ending just below the knee, a black silk camisole, a wide black, butter-leather belt, wide rectangular black onyx earrings with matching necklace, and black Prada pumps. Her hair was worn sleek and long. Having inherited her paternal grandmother's silky flyaway hair, it was best managed by simplicity. Her makeup was expertly applied to her honey bronzed complexion, accentuating her heart shaped face, high cheekbones and almond shaped, deep brown eyes. As she stood to leave she gave herself a final critical look in the cheval mirror which was in a corner of her bedroom. She was satisfied with the picture she presented. Long graceful neck, long slender limbs, and the curvaceous hips she and her three sisters shared. They were inherited from their mother, who in her fifties, could still cause men's eyes to dance when she entered a room. With a final glance, Amara picked up her black snakeskin attaché and headed for Mazrui Industries.

The company complex was located in the

Crystal City section of Arlington, Virginia, among very upscale retail stores and office buildings. This location was chosen specifically because of its proximity to Washington, D.C., and to Fairfax County, one of the nation's wealthiest leading high-tech corridors. Mazrui Industries was strategically placed between the two hot spots to take advantage of the best of two worlds without the headache of day to day gridlock. As she maneuvered her automobile through the city watching the effects of fall on the landscape, a feeling of excitement enveloped her. She really loved her work. She took great pride and pleasure in assisting companies with getting the very best from their employees. In the capacity of consultant and business owner she had the opportunity to do all of the things she loved: organizing, speaking, assessing, resolving conflicts, traveling, designing modules. Yes, she was ready! As she exited Jefferson Highway, the imposing structure that was Mazrui Industries came into view. The building was an architect's dream. A thoroughly modern edifice of glass and granite. It shouted wealth and stability. She drove into an underground parking area and took an elevator up to an entrance that was a glass enclosed courtyard bathed in a profusion of colorful perennials designed to give a feeling of spring freshness even in the most frigid winter. In the center of it all was a bronze thirty-foot replica of the West African Adinkra symbol of omnipotence.

It was all breathtaking, a fitting reflection of the man who was the powerful, innovative founder of this high stakes international trading company.

She walked into the reception area and stated, "Hello, I am Amara Terrell of Terrell and Associates."

The perky young cocoa colored receptionist wearing closely cropped natural hair, perfectly applied makeup and a dark nondescript business suit smiled and said, "Yes, Ms. Terrell, please go right up. Mrs. Rogers is waiting for you on the second floor, conference room A."

Amara entered the conference room and was met with a warm reception from Mrs. Rogers. Mary Rogers was a fiftyish Star Jones look-alike. She was a competent, sweet, no-nonsense lady married for thirty years with four adult children and three grands. She had been employed by Mazrui Industries from its inception.

"Ms. Terrell," she said, "I'm so very happy to see you again. Come in and meet the managers scheduled to see you today."

Amara smiled, shook Mrs. Rogers's hand and walked farther into the room and looked around. At the mahogany conference table seated in high-backed Italian Renaissance chairs, with expectant anticipation written on their faces, were the men and women with whom she would work. With a smile on her face, Amara took her place at the head of the table, placed her attaché in the chair beside her, unfolded her five-feet-eight-inch frame to its most elegant erect position and she was on!

Hours passed as Amara queried and listened. Others of her staff had arrived at the appointed time and the managers had been broken into triads and serious work had begun. At the end of the afternoon session, the conference room door opened. Amara felt a chill, causing her to look in the direction of the door. There he stood, a massive figure of solidly carved unyielding mahogany. A study in African royalty, elegance personified, impeccably dressed in a dark pinstriped Brioni suit, feet shod in black leather lace-up Testoni shoes, a pristine white shirt with French cuffs, black pearl cuff links and a gray silk tie. He was magnificent. For Amara a hush fell over the room. Through a haze she could hear voices saying, "Welcome back Mr. Mazrui."

She heard Mrs. Rogers say, "Good to see you, Mr. M. Let me introduce you to Ms. Terrell, the new consultant hired to refine some of our management techniques."

Hearing her name, Amara rose and started toward the powerful figure she saw in front of her.

As if in suspended animation Keino felt his heart speed up, his thoughts started to race. He had seen her bio and reference checks but he had not seen her. She was stunning. So graceful, so smoothly did she glide across the room that it placed him momentarily back at home in Africa watching a gazelle. A master of the art of emotional control, Keino steeled himself as he moved toward her with his own brand of commanding self-confidence. Their eyes froze simultaneously as they extended hands for the traditional greeting. While exchanging the customary pleasantries, the touch of their hands connected and without their knowing, so did their hearts, never to be separated again.

Keino removed his large sturdy hand from the soft touch of Amara's delicate one. As the earthly plane reclaimed her, so did the terrifying realization that it was not her work at Mazrui Industries that should cause her concern. It was indeed the powerful Mr. Keino Mazrui. She knew without doubt that her attraction to him was instantaneous. She had never in her life had her soul ravished by a look and a touch. She needed to run for her life as far away from Keino as possible, but her urge to run to him overpowered any other thought. She felt, more than heard, his cultivated East African tones filled with bass and bravado enfold her as he spoke. Amara was losing ground more quickly than she would ever have thought possible. At age twenty-eight, after having to call off a scheduled marriage to a financé who confessed that power was more important to him than anything, and that after they were married she would have to take a back seat to his climb up the corporate ladder, she promised herself that she would never again become involved with a wannabe power broker. Yet, here she was, so hopelessly attracted to a man who had proven himself to be such a master power broker that she could not see straight, hear clearly, nor stand still. Dear God, it took all of her self-control to stand in one spot and attempt to look and sound normal.

Not only was he a power broker, but he was foreign born with foreign sensibilities. Taking in his authoritative stance, and his imperious demeanor, she knew that the way he appeared did not end with his physical stature, but permeated every fiber of his being. She suspected that his idea of a woman's place was prehistoric. She could imagine him wanting a woman who knew her place; a covered up, quiet, out-of-the-way baby-making machine. She was going to be none of those things. She was not going to subjugate herself or her dreams, to or for anyone. As the thoughts raced through her mind, she had to mentally laugh at herself. She didn't even know Keino, and already she had given him a value system and turned him into an ogre with the power to change her life.

Keino was fighting his own battle with self-control. To him her voice was like silk. It was so low and sensual, it sent ripples through him. He could not remember ever having experienced such a torrent of feeling. *What is wrong with you?* He said to himself. All of this heat over an American woman. *Come on, Keino, your jet lag is beginning to make you come unglued. This preoccupation with finding a wife has pickled your brain and scrambled your hormones. Yes you need to find a wife, but not a plaything, and an American is definitely for play. You know the drill. You know what many Americans perceive you to be because of your heritage. You don't have time to explain to anyone that you are not an unsocialized creature, ready to throw your woman in a room and only allow her to exit to give birth.* The assumptions some Americans have would be laughable if they weren't so foolish.

Recovering momentarily from the warmth of her touch, and his rambling thoughts, his eyes studied her with what she perceived as dangerous intent. They exchanged a final glance, then he turned and was gone.

Amara pulled herself together and began gathering her materials as she prepared for her departure. Terrell and Associates' staff members had left earlier, rushing back to the office to assess, evaluate, reevaluate and design based on the day's findings.

As Amara packed her briefcase, a wave of warmth flooded her as she relived the events of the day. Things had gone well. Not only was her competence not questioned but her skill, and that of her staff, was continually lauded as the process she had designed unfolded throughout the day. Another thought occurred to her; her sister Afiya had been right. It wasn't the work she wasn't prepared for; it was the fiercely sexual energy and raw power emanating from one Mr. Keino Mazrui. Fleeting thoughts of the vision of African royalty she had met earlier, filled her with a longing she had never experienced. The idea of having him touch her again, even in the harmless gesture of a handshake, sent her reeling to the point of having to put her palm to her head to steady herself. Every thought of him increased the temperature in the room. She decided to hurry. She really needed to temporarily remove herself from reminders of the intensely virile CEO of Mazrui Industries.

Once again the door opened. This time it was Mary Rogers. "Ms. Terrell, I thought the session went very well today. It is clear that you will be able to quickly get a handle on the areas in which the managers could use the most assistance. We are so happy to have you working with us."

"Thank you Mrs. Rogers. I really appreciate all of the preliminary work you did to make this day happen."

"You are so very welcome! On your way out you've got one more stop to make. Mr. Mazrui would like to see you in his office for a short de-briefing."

Amara could feel herself start to panic as she stood stoically, continuing to listen to the pleasant explanation Mrs. Rogers offered as to why she, Amara, had to walk into the fiery furnace which was Keino's office.

Mrs. Rogers continued, "We didn't expect him back so soon. He has been out of the country in Kenya visiting his parents, and checking on matters at the company headquarters in Nairobi. He just flew in this morning. His office is the top floor. The private elevator is through this door." She pointed to Amara's left. "Once you are through the door, turn right." Amara's unsettled look prompted Mrs. Rogers to say reassuringly, "Ms. Terrell, his bark is worse than his bite. He really is a very kind man. He is driven, I will admit, and certainly obsessed when he wants to get something done, but his heart is pure gold."

It then registered with Amara that the anxiety she was feeling must have been written quite clearly on her face. She apologized to Mrs. Rogers for the stunned look, and for her hesitation. She explained that although she was not expecting to present a debriefing today she would gladly adhere to her client's request.

With this added dimension to today's events, Amara took a deep breath to calm her racing heart, and quietly finished collecting her things. As she walked into the elevator and pressed the appropriate button, she nervously ran her fingers through her hair. She told herself to relax, to remember that Keino Mazrui was just a man, albeit the most hauntingly sexual, dangerously arrogant, powerfully built, devastatingly handsome man she had ever met—but still a man.

"Amara Terrell," she said aloud to herself, "you may have been out of the male/female game for a while, five years to be exact, but you are not a teenager. You are a competent professional woman; pull yourself together."

Just as she completed her solitary verbal tirade, the elevator door opened and she was astounded by the visual picture she encountered

This office space was unlike any she had ever seen. As she stepped off the elevator, stark white walls covered with contemporary African and African-American art immediately gave her the feeling of being in a most exclusive, well appointed art gallery. As she looked up she could see that where a roof should have been there were skylights everywhere. In the middle of the long expanse, which was a hallway, was set the most beautiful antique French desk; on it was a large Japanese vase filled with tall stately gladiolus. A valet stood, waiting to announce her arrival. The attendant saw Amara, smiled and said, "Mr. Mazrui is waiting, Ms. Terrell, please enter the first door to your right."

Amara smiled and said, "Thank you."

When she reached the door to Keino's private sanctuary she hesitated, trying futilely to calm her erratic pulse, and then knocked twice softly. She heard that very distinctive cultured Kenyan voice say "Please, come." When she opened the door she knew she was in the presence of a man who could not be a mere mortal. He had to be an incarnation of the Egyptian god Osiris. She had seen wealth, but this was more. The decor of his office was not just about a display of wealth. This was the signature of a man who had only known affluence. He was so at home in this world as he stood motionless in the middle of the room, amid fine silks, priceless antiques and collections of objects from all over the world. This office with its brass chandelier, highly polished hardwood floors, Persian rugs, mahogany wet bar, views of breathtaking vistas, rarefied tranquility and sense of total seclusion all belonged to this man.

One could tell that he was born to this display of African and European opulence. It would not have been possible for him to have been surrounded by any less.

Chapter 4

Keino stood riveted as Amara entered his domain. The picture she painted would remain in his mind forever. His eyes became the photographic lens of a high-powered camera as he captured frame by frame every elegant step she took, every movement of her curvaceous hips, the swaying of her hair and the captivating beauty of her face as her smile sent electrical currents through his highly charged body. It was a masterful seduction, and she had not even touched him. Her silken tones floated toward him as she said, "Hello again, Mr. Mazrui. I was told you wanted to have me brief you concerning today's events."

"Yes, Ms. Terrell, please come in and have a seat." He directed her to a section of the room which had been designed to look like a replica of a grand salon complete with French doors and a marble fireplace. The panoramic views were continued in this area of the room. There were two white silk sofas with an intricately carved coffee table separating them. Atop the coffee table, creat-

ing a tablescape, was a collection of miniature
Benin bronze sculptures. The walls were graced
with shelves of leather-bound volumes, and ster-
ling silver framed photos were everywhere. The
amateur interior designer in her was enthralled by
the beautiful arrangements of furniture, books and
objets d'art that surrounded her. She sat gingerly
on one of the sofas, crossed her long legs and tried
to cool the disturbing quakes she felt riding like
tumultuous waves through her body. She was trying desperately to hold on to her fragile control.
This man was wreaking havoc with her peace of
mind. Keino spoke again. His voice was warm,
smooth, and deep. She could feel the vibrato in
the pit of her stomach.

"Ms. Terrell, may I have some refreshments
brought to you?"

She answered with a faint tremor in her voice
that only she could hear. "Thank you, no, I'm just
fine. I really don't want to take up too much of
your time, Mr. Mazrui. Though this was an un-
planned briefing, there are things I can and would
like to report."

"Please do Ms. Terrell. I am anxious to hear."

Keino found himself utterly entranced by this
woman. Absolutely drawn to her. He knew he
could have waited for a later briefing but he found
himself needing an excuse to see her again, to see
if his senses had fooled him before when he was so
taken by the sight, sound, and smell of her. There
was something very different about this very beautiful woman, though it was not her beauty that intrigued him, for his world was filled with beautiful
women. Was it her confidence, her poise, her elegance, her intelligence, her eyes? Something, something about her pulled at him. He needed to know

if it was jet lag, his loneliness, or if it was just Ms. Amara Terrell. He told himself that he would find out, but keep his distance, because after all, she was an American woman. She could have no place in the realities of his life.

Amara began her overview of the day's events surprising him with her thoroughness and her insightful analytical way of so quickly sizing up his managers and their particular managerial styles. She surprised herself with her ability to perform efficiently and professionally in spite of the raging fire building inside her every time she looked at Keino, or was close enough to melt into the aromatic fragrance of his cologne. She could hear a small voice say, *Careful, Amara.*

After listening to her explain to him in detail how her company could assist his in the area of professional development, he was even more taken with her presence, and not just as a professional but as a woman. As she spoke he watched the outline of her full lips, wondering if they were as soft as they appeared. He found himself periodically glancing at the base of her slender honey colored throat, wanting to feel its warmth on his lips. The first time she sat on the sofa his peripheral vision had not missed the tasteful way in which she had crossed the legs he longed to touch. Where had his mind gone? This was not a common practice for him. Here was Keino Mazrui under the guise of discussing business, fantasizing about making passionate love to a woman he did not even know. No woman had ever had this effect on him. This was a woman he knew did not share his values. He was not one to waste time, money, or energy. What was he doing?

He came to himself as he heard her say, "Mr.

Mazrui, I hope you will be pleased with the work once it's completed."

He cleared his throat and in spite of the strange and torturous thoughts racing through his mind his vibrato tones did not fail him as he said, "I am certain your work will be more than satisfactory, Ms. Terrell. If you are in need of anything to make the project go more smoothly, please do not hesitate to let Mary Rogers know. She will get whatever you need." As Keino spoke he bore into her with his unconsciously seductive stare. He was smitten, that he knew.

Amara felt as though her body had been engulfed in flames. She wanted to fan, she wanted to remove her jacket, she wanted to run, she wanted a cool breeze, she wanted a shower, she wanted this man. She was not giving in to these feelings—he could not be her man! He came closer and looked deeply into her eyes, waiting for a response. Haltingly Amara answered, "Mrs. Rogers has already been extremely helpful."

She took a deep unsteady breath, turned and started preparing to leave. At that moment Keino touched her shoulder and with a light but firm grasp turned her to face him. "Ms. Terrell," he said, "I don't want to appear presumptious but I'm very interested in how you came to be called Amara. My mother is Ethiopian and your name is one used quite frequently among the Amharic people. In fact, I have an aunt named Amara, my mother's sister."

"My name?" Amara stammered. The headiness caused by his touch had clouded her thinking. "My name. Well"—she took a cleansing breath—"my parents have been in love with the continent of Africa since their college days. My three sisters and I were given African names. My Ethiopian name was given to me because it belonged to a college roommate of my mother's."

"It is a very lovely name," Keino replied, "very appropriate for its owner. May I use it? Since we will be working closely together perhaps we can drop the formalities."

He extended his hand and grasped hers tenderly but firmly, thinking how velvety soft she was, and said, "Now, let's start over. Hello, Amara, my name is Keino. I am very happy to meet you."

She leaned her head back and gazed into his eyes, laughed and said, "I am very happy to meet you, too, Keino."

He bent forward slightly and almost whispered, "In order to consummate our newfound informality, please accompany me to a very comfortable little spot I enjoy. It is not very far from here and we can sit and talk in a more relaxed atmosphere and get to know one another in an environment that is less stilted. I think that will not only help us, but the more relaxed we are with one another the more smoothly our work will progress."

Keino amazed himself. He heard his own voice and was astounded at the blatant ploy he presented just to spend more time with the enchanting Ms. Terrell. He hoped she bought it no matter how transparent. Something about her would not let him part from her. He was buying time while continually telling himself he could not become involved.

Amara hesitated. There was certainly a part of her that wanted to spend a lot of time with this man, but he was her employer no matter how earthshakingly gorgeous. As she tried to make a decision in a split second Keino said, "Amara, shall we go? You can ride with me and I will bring you back to your car."

Amara looked into those eyes, heard that voice and responded, "All right, Keino, lead the way."

The two silently rode the elevator down to Keino's private parking garage. Once in the garage, with an array of luxury automobiles from which to choose, Keino opened the door for Amara to enter a sleek new, steel gray Jaguar. Amara entered the gunmetal gray cocoon and was immediately enveloped in smells of new leather and the woodsy scent she knew by now to be Keino's fragrance. She sighed deeply as Keino slid into the seat next to her. He turned the key, pushed a button and the sounds of Miles Davis playing a piece from "Sketches in Spain" came lightly through the state-of-the-art speaker system. Keino skillfully wheeled the car into the street. The sleek, smooth, silver Jaguar streaked down the highway as confidently as the four-legged creature for which it was named, purring as every gear set itself in motion. The sophisticated passengers sat in companionable solitude engulfed by the rays of the setting sun.

They headed toward the downtown area and within minutes were in front of an elegant old building which had been refurbished as a private club for people of means to entertain themselves and their friends. As Keino slowed to a stop in front of the building, a parking attendant appeared and opened the door for Amara.

Keino handed the attendant his keys and he placed his hand on the small of Amara's back as he led her up the stairs to the awning draped entrance. The heat from his palm radiated sensuously throughout her lower extremities. Touching her left him wanting to experience much more of the lovely creature walking beside him. They continued walking, each lost in pleasurable but conflicted thoughts.

As they entered the building Keino was greeted warmly by staff and patrons alike. The main sitting room was decorated to resemble a medieval castle with high stone fireplaces, high-back chairs and overstuffed sofas. He led Amara to a private sitting room for which he, and others who wanted to do so, paid extra to reserve.

The room was very cozy. A fireplace blazed brightly as Keino walked over and touched the sound system to elicit the mellow sounds of Grover Washington Jr. Amara took a seat in the wing-back chair that matched the one where Keino moved to sit, after she had made herself comfortable. As if on command, a gentleman appeared dressed in formal attire carrying a silver tray and on it Keino's favorite port and two beautiful crystal glasses. He placed the tray on a table in the center of the two chairs and bowed his exit. Keino thanked the exiting waiter.

With the fire blazing, music softly playing and lighting adjusted for twilight, Amara and Keino sipped their drinks and bathed in the sensuousness of the moment. Keino was the first to speak. "This is my hideaway when I am working in Virginia. I hope you like it. It is peaceful, and one can breathe easily here."

As he spoke, Amara watched his mahogany skin molded tautly across his face. It was so beautiful. She wanted to touch it with her fingertips and stroke its smoothness. She wondered how his cheeks would feel next to hers if they were to embrace. She was at a loss to explain these feelings, they were so new. Pulled from her reverie by Keino's melodic tones, unsure as to what had been said, she responded with, "I am sorry Mr. Mazrui. What did you say?"

"First of all, I'd like to hear you say 'Keino' outside of the office. I thought we had agreed to dispense with that particular formality."

Amara laughed. "I won't forget again," she said, intrigued by his insistence upon a less formal connection. "You just aren't the kind of man people call by his first name. You look like you need a title before you are addressed. It takes some getting used to, but I have been known to be a quick study."

Amara said this with a twinkle in her eye that captivated and delighted Keino. To show his pleasure, his smiling face burst into deep velvety laughter, which rolled in waves over Amara as she sat startled by the unexpected gaiety she had elicited in him. "Am I that formidable?" Keino asked, still with the remnants of a smile lingering on his lips.

"I am sure that you know that you are," Amara responded, with an approving smile.

"Well, if I am formidable, Amara, you are enchanting. You know that in the legends of old Ethiopia, which was then called Abyssinia, Amara was the name for paradise?"

"So I've been told. It is also Ki Swahili for urgent business," Amara added. "My father always jokes that my name is fitting because my birth was so quick. He says I rushed out of paradise ready to take care of business." The statement caught them both up in a gale of laughter. They found themselves enjoying an easy comfortable moment, a fleeting moment of camaraderie laced with undeniable sexual tension.

Keino found himself wanting to know more and

more about this woman, while reminding himself to keep his emotional distance. It wasn't an obsession, but it was, he was sure, as close as he would ever come to one. He wanted to know who she really was, her likes, dislikes, stresses, frustrations. He really wanted to know this elegant creature who was sitting leisurely across from him crossing a pair of the longest, most exquisitely shaped legs he had ever had the pleasure of visually devouring. At that moment, her origin of birth was of little concern. He had no idea of the turmoil Amara was experiencing as she remained deceptively calm, reminding herself that he couldn't be the one.

"Tell me, Amara," Keino stated with more control than he felt, "are you all business?"

"No, no," protested Amara, "that's my older sister Alexandra Adana. Attorney par excellence. Clearly on her way to a judgeship. She is all business. I like to think that I enjoy my life. I love my work. Building my small company has been a labor of love. I have been able to handpick a wonderful staff. We work together like a loving family. I enjoy interior design as a hobby. I read a great deal, I travel, and I enjoy life.

"And now that you've peeped into my life Keino," she said with a gentle softness, "I'd love to know, what makes life happen for you?"

Keino looked deeply into Amara's eyes, obsidian on black pearl. He was still basking in the sensuousness of her voice when he said, "I don't believe anyone has ever asked that of me before."

Pensively he stated, "Life happens for me when I am productive, when I am building and when I am in the bosom of a loving family." As if coming back to consciousness, he said, "I am just getting settled here in Virginia. I'll be here permanently for another three years, then back to Kenya as my home base. I just purchased a house, and it is so bare you can hear echoes," he said with a smile in his voice. "Since you are an interior designer, your expertise would be greatly appreciated."

The thought of doing anything in his home sent tingling sensations throughout Amara's body. She quickly responded. "Oh, no, I said amateur. I can help you, though. My sister Cassandra is a pro. She has one of the hottest design houses in the city, and she has a very impressive client list. I'll have her give Mrs. Rogers a call and she can, as they say, 'hook you up.' "

The sensuality in his voice was unmistakable as he said, "Trust me, I need to be hooked up."

After scrumptious appetizers and port, peppered with more delightful conversation and much laughter, Keino took Amara back to her car, where they thanked each other for a pleasant evening and parted with a professional warmth, leaving them both wanting more.

As each drove to their separate residences it was clear that they had connected in a way that was more intense than either had anticipated. Amara smiled, thinking of how wrong she had been to have had uneasy feelings about Keino. Yes, he was a hard taskmaster and the consummate businessman, but he was also compassionate, kind, bright, wonderfully humorous and one of the most magnificent physical beings she had ever met. She knew she had to be careful because he also unearthed feelings in her she had never experienced.

As Keino drove home, his only thought was how different Amara was from any other woman he had ever known. What the difference was he could not articulate. He promised himself he would soon find out. In that moment he knew that no matter how hard he fought to keep his emotional distance, Amara's essence had already seeped into the fabric of his soul.

Chapter 5

NAIROBI, KENYA

Judge Garsen Mazrui spoke very crisply to the visitor in his chambers. "Ali, it is not at all in line with our traditions for you to come here, first without your father, and then to badger me about the marriage plans of my son Keino to your sister Makena. This is a matter which will be settled by my wife and me, your parents, Keino and Makena. I am not discussing any of the particulars of the matrimonial arrangements with you."

Ali Rono, a tall, slightly built man with haunted eyes, warily observed the judge as he waited for him to complete his lecture on the matrimonial mores of Kenyan society. When it was clear to him that he could speak, he started slowly and apologetically. "Judge Mazrui, please accept my humblest apologies, if I have offended you. I am, as you know, Makena's eldest brother, and in my father's absence, she comes to me with all of her concerns about this matter and expresses feelings of complete rejection. It does not please me to watch my sister suffer as she waits for your son to honor his obligations. I came today to see if there is anything that can be done to save my sister the embarrassment she is facing. I again apologize for the break in the traditional form, but as a man who has himself on occasion not adhered to the traditional path, I had hoped that you would understand and allow me this liberty."

Judge Mazrui responded angrily, "Regardless of the paths I have or have not chosen, you have no right, at this time, and in this way, to speak for your father. As for me allowing you liberty, you have taken far too many liberties in this matter. I will not be pressured by you. You are an arrogant, disrespectful young man who has overstepped his bounds. You may leave now and when I see you again you will come to me in a more appropriate manner. The Mazrui family's dealings in this matter have been honorable and I will not have it appear otherwise. Your innuendoes about embarrassment and breach of promise have no place in any discussion with me concerning my son. Am I clear?"

Ali nodded his agreement, turned and left feeling as though he had been dismissed like a wayward child. He mentally vowed that the Mazrui family would not get away with this treatment of his precious sister. With that thought in mind, he started the journey to his family home to assure his sister that in time, all would be well.

The drive from Nairobi to the Rono family homestead was forty-five minutes, giving Ali Rono ample time to contemplate a number of methods of exacting from the Mazrui family the justice he felt his family deserved.

As he drove, the beauty of the Nairobi countryside did not reflect his mood. Kenya, known the world over for its beauty, was no exception today. The variety of flora, fauna, and wildlife made it a paradise on earth. Instead of feeling exhilarated by the wonder which surrounded him, Ali Rono felt suffocated by his inability to navigate the complex underpinnings of the culture of his birth.

His father Jomo Rono had reared his children to adhere to the old ways. His father even had more than one wife, a custom clearly fading in deference to the onslaught of Christian monogamy. The confusion of being reared in traditional ways and yet having to struggle to incorporate the new mores into daily life was causing Ali much frustration. Ali and Makena Rono were the children of Jomo Rono, a wealthy Kenyan businessman, and Apiyo Rono, his highly ambitious first wife. Both children had been openly spoiled by their mother, because they were, after all, much to her delight, the firstborn son and daughter, in that order, of Jomo Rono. Their mother expected everyone she knew to pay homage to her precious seed. Jomo indulged his wife, and Ali and Makena grew up believing that the world did indeed owe them the desires of their hearts. They were both equally impossible to live with when thwarted.

Ali drove into the Rono compound, dreading having to face his spoiled, unhappy sister; but he loved her and was bound by duty to protect her. Ali wheeled his black, late model, Mercedes-Benz sedan onto the well tended grounds of his home. There were three stately homes on the property. The largest home was occupied by the patriarch of the family, Jomo Rono, and his son Ali and his two younger brothers, eighteen- and nineteen-year-old college students, who were currently studying abroad. These were the sons of his father's second wife. The other homes belonged to the Rono wives and their female children. Each wife had one daughter. Ali's second sister was also living abroad.

When Ali entered his sister Makena's home he found her lounging on a plush, maroon colored sofa in the drawing room; she appeared to be resting. Her eyes were closed and her breathing shallow. He entered the spacious open room and gently touched Makena to get her attention. Makena slowly opened her eyes, smiled and said, "Hello, my brother. You were gone for such a long time, I was worried." She stretched in the most feline way a human being could manage and queried, "How did the meeting go with my future father-in-law?"

Ali began speaking more rapidly than usual. "Makena, my darling sister, this slight to our family has gone on long enough. In days gone by, Keino Mazrui would have been brought before the Council of Elders and made to answer for his indiscretions. He would not have been allowed to get away with holding hostage the lives of our family and therefore our community. You know that."

"Yes, Ali, I know; thank you so much for caring about me, your little sister. I am at a loss as to what to do. I feel so humiliated. I received a call this morning from Keino saying that he will be in Nairobi in a few days and we should talk. Somehow I do not feel as though he is coming to set our date. I just don't know what to do." Makena then allowed rehearsed tears to fall, painting the picture of dejection for her enraged brother.

Taking Makena in his arms, Ali said, "I vow on the graves of our ancestors, Keino will not get away with this shame he has brought on our family."

Makena's smile was unseen by her angry brother.

Chapter 6

James and Ana Terrell watched lovingly as their four daughters engaged in a lively discussion around the dinner table. This Sunday afternoon ritual was one they tried to adhere to at least once a month. It gave them an opportunity to stay physically connected to their daughters even though they spoke with them frequently by telephone. The sermon at church today had been the catalyst which sparked this spirited discussion.

James Terrell looked at his wife, while his daughters' words were flying around the table, and commented, "They are the four most beautiful young women in this city."

Ana, his wife of thirty-five years, responded with a smile in her voice. "Why, James, I'm surprised you didn't say the most beautiful in the world—or certainly in the state."

James Terrell was an extremely tall, erect six feet six inches. He possessed a very handsome carmel colored face which always held a ready smile. His soft wavy hair had developed one luminous streak of silver which started at his widow's peak and stopped in the middle of his head. His long lean frame had been a necessary ingredient in his success during his college days at Morehouse, where he had been a star basketball player. He had gained entrance to Atlanta's renowned Morehouse college on an academic scholarship, but continued to pursue basketball, the sport he had loved since junior high school.

After graduation, James had entered Washington, D.C.'s prestigious Howard University with a dual agenda. He expected, one, to complete masters and doctoral degrees in Political Science, and two, to woo into marriage the beautiful Ana Marie Chatfield, a Washington, D.C. native whom he had dated while she was a student on the Spelman University campus in Atlanta, Georgia. Since Ana had returned home after graduation and also enrolled in Howard's graduate department to study for a doctorate in Psychology, he felt his chances were beyond good. He had prevailed, and here they sat thirty-five years and four daughters later, enjoying a Sunday afternoon ritual. As he looked at his wife, she was still as pretty as ever. Café au lait skin still smooth and unlined. Her naturally henna colored hair had been lightened in streaks to camouflage any hints of premature graying. She still wore it hanging loosely around her shoulders; her tall graceful body was still trim and toned after four births and an accumulation of years, because of her high energy and her love of aerobic exercise.

As James and Ana shared their intimate moment Adana spotted them and remarked aloud,

"Oh, girls, we've lost Mom and Dad. They are in their own world again."

Conversation stopped as they all focused on their parents. Afiya, the art gallery owner, spoke. "One of these days I am going to have that kind of love and partnership in my life."

"Yes, we all are," Amara chimed in.

Adana, the attorney, almost yelled, "Speak for yourself. I am not looking."

"Yes, Adana, we know," they said almost in unison.

Cassandra, ever the inquisitor concerning personal matters, verbalized a question all of the daughters pondered often. "Mom and Dad, for the one hundredth time, how do you two do it? In a day and age when divorce is as common as a cold, how do you keep the love sparking?"

The older Terrells looked at each other. They were beaming with a contentment that comes from a life of living and growing individually and as a unit. James spoke. "Girls, I have said to you often and this piece of James Edward Terrell philosophy still has not changed: Before you choose your mates, make sure to the best of your ability, you know who you are. Know your bottom lines, your likes, dislikes, frustration levels, values, things about which you cannot compromise. Your companion has to be a reflection of your best self. It's much easier when the time comes to compromise, to do so with the better part of your soul. Trust yourselves, be able to trust your partner with your life. Forge a friendship that is unsurpassed. Look for like values concerning the big ticket items like the earning and handling of money, child rearing. I know it sounds like a lot but when it's right it comes together in the twinkling of an eye. And," he said with a slow smile, "a little chemistry never hurt."

At that moment, Ana playfully swatted her husband's shoulder with a light tap and said with a pointed glance laced with a smile, "Sweethearts, do not worry, you will all find your loves, even you, Adana. You've seen love all of your lives, because God knows, I do love your father in spite of himself."

James Edward Terrell at that moment reached over, encased his wife in his long, strong, loving arms and kissed her ever so gently and in a style much more chaste than he was feeling, but he remembered that they had an audience. Each daughter in turn and in her own style thanked James and Ana for the words of wisdom, and for just being.

"All right, my pets," James Terrell said with pride, "catch your mother and me up on your lives. Tell us what you want us to know, and what you don't want us to know," he said, laughing loudly.

"James, what am I going to do with you," chastised Ana.

"Just love me, sweetie," he responded.

"Mom and Dad, stop it," said Adana, feigning embarrassment. "Parents just don't act like you people," she said, smiling. "Let me share my news before we have to send you two to your room for misconduct."

The entire family shared warm comfortable laughter at Adana's reprimand of her parents.

"OK, everyone," Adana began, "word is that I'm being considered for a judgeship."

Delight was evident in everyone's eyes. Each person spoke to Adana about her worthiness, her competence and their pride in, and love for, her.

Adana finished with, "The rumor mill is silent on when this should happen, but I look forward to the challenge."

Afiya spoke next. "Business is really expanding. It's booming. There is a real rush on African and African-American art these days. I'm working now with Garvis Lane on his one man show. The reception will be huge and his installations are quite an undertaking so I'm busy and I'm happy."

Cassandra joined the discussion. "Everyone here knows I am in my world when I'm decorating. Creating beauty and harmony in any environment. New clients are coming from everywhere with the resources to just let me flow. You know I am in heaven."

Amara added, "My new contract is going very well." As she spoke, visions of Keino Mazrui cascaded through her mind like water falling from a mountain stream. Her memories of him were so vivid. Since the day they met thoughts of him had never left the shadowy recesses of her mind. Where did those thoughts come from? she wondered. As she resurfaced and entered again mentally into the bosom of her family, she remembered her promise to Keino.

"Cassandra, through my new client I may have some work for you. The CEO of Mazrui Industries, remember the one I had so many reservations about? Well he has just moved here temporarily from Nairobi and needs a decorator. I told him he needs your touch."

"Hey, thanks, sis; tell me about him. This could be fun."

"Well, I know very little about him, really. He's Kenyan and Ethiopian, has a transcontinental firm, is highly respected by his staff, has exquisite taste, is very bright, and he is very arrogant in an appealing sort of way."

All eyes were on Amara as she described Keino and it was apparent to all listening that she had developed more than a professional interest in Mr. Keino Mazrui. Afiya was the first to rush in with questions. "Is he single? Is he fine?"

"Yes on both counts," Amara stated thoughtfully.

Now it was Cassandra's turn. "Oh, baby girl, when are you going to make your move?"

"What move?" Amara answered, startled by the question. "This is strictly business; besides, he is an African man, African aristocracy no less, who probably has a very different set of values than mine."

Now it was Adana's turn. "You don't make a believable witness. Amara, everyone here saw that faraway look in your eyes when you were describing Mr. Wonderful. That man struck a nerve, sweetie. And besides, you don't really know him yet. Don't assume you can read him."

Ana Terrell spoke. Although she agreed with the others about Amara's clear interest in this man, she felt Amara needed rescuing at that moment. "All right girls, give Amara a chance to hear her own thunder. I promise you, darlings, when the time comes none of us will have to tell her what we see or hear."

James looked on, silently marveling at the feminine process.

Amara wondered if she had already heard the thunder. Had it come in the form of Mr. Mahogany Granite himself? No one, not even her ex-fiancé, had caused her to question herself or her feelings.

Chapter 7

Keino's doorbell rang and he jumped, startled for a moment until he remembered where he was and that he was expecting his brothers. They were arriving from Kenya on business and to relax for a few days. The doorbell rang just as he was deep in thought about the tempting Ms. Amara Terrell. He found himself thinking of her more and more frequently. It probably did not help that she had been in the office for a few weeks working with Mrs. Rogers and a number of Mazrui mangers to finish the project evaluations. He almost felt pained whenever he saw her. Something about her drew him in like the proverbial moth. When she passed him in the halls, her scent lingered in his nostrils. It had not been unusual for his body to become rigid at the sight of her.

He drew himself up from his wing-back chair, one of the few pieces of furniture in his newly acquired home. When he opened the door, three faces as handsome and as rugged as his, greeted him. They all eagerly embraced one another in the way that brothers who love each other and who have lived a lifetime of adventures together, do.

Keino's brothers, like him, were well educated, from the prestigious St. Mary's in Nairobi to the finest universities England and the United States could offer. Judge Mazrui insisted that his sons have a global sense of African manhood in order to hopefully make lifelong connections which would be with them always in their business, and social lives. For this training they had all matriculated through Atlanta, Georgia's Morehouse College for a portion of their undergraduate studies.

Aman, the second son, was given an Amharic name meaning peace and he was indeed a peaceful man. Soft-spoken, a man of few words, very direct and to the point when he did speak. All of the Mazrui men were tall. Aman was no exception. All were muscular but Aman was leaner than his brothers, built more like his mother's people. He and his younger brother Kaleb had more of their mother's bronze skin tone brushed by their father's mahogany, but their features held none of their mother's softness that was reserved for Keino and Kamau. Aman was a physician, a cardiac specialist in private practice. The third son, Kamau, was a corporate attorney, powerful in and out of the courtroom. He and Keino shared a similar temperament. Kamau worked as the lead partner in the firm their father founded. Since their father's judgeship it was he, Kamau, who had made sure that the law firm remained the best in Nairobi. Kaleb, the youngest of the group, had a personality that could light up any room, always with the ready quip and adventurous spirit. He was well suited for his chosen profession, flying commercial jets both at home and abroad. When called upon, he often flew the two family jets. He had loved soaring above the clouds since he was a child.

Aman spoke first. "Well, big brother, I see from the looks of things we needed to come to rescue you. Man, you've been here a few months and you still haven't found furniture."

Keino smiled, inclined his head and said, "Good to see you too, Aman."

Kaleb the jokester jumped in. "Hey, man, get off big brother's back. You know he's waiting for Makena, his betrothed, to come to put her own stamp on this place. Aren't you, big brother?"

"Probably not," the insightful Kamau stated. "You're not moving too swiftly in that direction, are you, Keino?"

"My brothers, my brothers. Did you really come all this way just to dissect my life?" asked the protesting Keino. "Come on now, fellows, come in, relax. I do have beds, tables, a few chairs, and electronics. What more could you want?" With that question they all laughed, bringing back memories of shared laughter as children.

As they all found spaces to deposit luggage, and seats to rest well-traveled bodies, Keino spoke, "So, my inquisitive brothers, what is the word from home? How are things?"

Kaleb offered, "I've been flying Dad around quite a lot over the last few months and something is amiss with our father. I can't put my finger on it, but something is weighing heavily on his mind."

"I agree," added Kamau. "In the office, when he comes through, his demeanor has left a bit to be desired. I'd say he's distracted and very preoccupied.

Fortunately he is merely a figurehead these days. If we needed his skill or expertise we'd be in trouble. His attention just isn't there. It doesn't seem to affect his rulings on the bench, though. He's as efficient as ever in that arena."

Aman spoke. "You are very right about the sometimes distracted behavior. Kayla and I had Mom and Dad over for dinner three nights ago, and even the children could not totally absorb him as they are known to do. Our mother seemed a bit concerned about him."

"Did she say something?" asked Keino.

Aman responded, "No, it wasn't what she said. You know that look Mother gets when she is concerned about family, especially our father."

"Yes," they all said in unison.

Kamau added, "To the world at large they appear to be the genteel 'in-charge' couple, but we know when something is just a little off center."

After absorbing all that he had heard, Keino felt a twinge of guilt and hoped that his father's distracted demeanor had nothing to do with the complications surrounding his impending marriage, but he was sure it did. Forcing the distressing thoughts from his mind he said, "And so, my brothers, we will, I am sure, find out soon the mystery to Dad's change in behavior—meantime give me an update on wives and children."

Aman spoke, "Ah, yes, wives and children, indeed the joy of life. Before Kayla and I had our sons, I thought life could not be more perfect. I was wrong; children add another dimension to living. I used to wonder when we were children why I would catch Mom smiling as she stared at us. Now I know why."

As Aman talked about his family, basking in the pride he felt, Keino kept having flashes of Amara's smile, the tilt of her head when she laughed, the smoothness of silk in her voice, the sensuality in her stride. *My God*, he thought to himself, *you want that woman.* He cleared his throat and said, "And my brother, how is my beautiful sister Kayla?"

His brother Aman responded pridefully, "As beautiful and as high-strung as ever. I never know who I am coming home to, but I enjoy the mystery. Kayla is my eternal adventure."

Kamau spoke up, "And you need adventure brother. If you were any more serious we would have to canonize you."

Kaleb, the resident jester, started laughter that was contagious; as Aman sat looking stoic, gales of laughter from his siblings rang throughout the house. When the riotous laughter had ceased, Aman spoke again. "I am very satisfied that I allowed parental wisdom to prevail in my decision to marry Kayla. Our parents knew the characteristics of the woman I would need. They are all embodied in Kayla."

Keino asked, "Is she still teaching at the university?"

"Only part time; the boys, three, four, and six, take up most of her time. Though she could have full-time help she chooses to be a very hands-on mother, reminiscent of our mother."

Kamau interjected, "Oh, yes, my brothers, the right woman can be a joyous gift. Though I have only been married a short while, I can already feel the effects of my wife on my life. I am looking forward to adding fatherhood to my repertoire. Yasmin is beautiful, and a fierce law partner. I enjoy watch-

ing her skillfully interpret the law. I must say, I would
not want to be her adversary."

They all shared the humor of the possibility of
Kamau being in such a situation.

"Well," said Kaleb, "since we are all sharing our
joys, you, my brothers, need to be the first to know
that Mara and I are expecting our fourth baby this
summer."

Congratulatory remarks went around ending
with Keino saying, "Man, Kaleb, as much as you fly,
how do you have time?"

"Ah, my brother, when I am home I make my
time count."

This time the laughter was uncontrollable. As it
subsided, Aman cleared his throat and pointedly
asked, "Keino when are we to attend your wedding? You and Makena have been betrothed. You
have let the time pass and have not formally released her. Her older brother Ali is becoming
quite hostile about the length of time you have
taken. I am hearing the rumors. I am sure that
soon our parents will start to feel the pressure if
they haven't already. You know first-wife Rono is
very ambitious, and she thinks that to marry into
our family would be a feather in her cap, and she
will not stop until she has it."

Keino responded, "I have explained to our parents that I am not ready. Makena is lovely, but she
is not for me. I want what I see in your households.
I may be the elder brother, but this time I am not
the example to follow. I have told Makena pri-
vately that she is free to marry someone else. So far
she won't hear of it, and frankly I have been so
busy with work I have not taken this whole fiasco
seriously until now. I know a decision must come
soon. I can stall Father no longer. With the family

reputation and honor at stake he will have my head!"

"You can count on that," stated Kamau. "It must be Makena or someone."

Chapter 8

After several days of work and play, the brothers bid one another farewell and Kaleb piloted the trio back to Kenya, leaving Keino alone to continue the contemplation of his future. The thoughts uppermost in his mind were of Amara. He could not shake his need to touch, taste, and possess her. He wanted her with every fiber of his being.

There was a meeting soon which he scheduled with top level managers—and Amara—to review the implementation of the manual Terrell and Associates had developed. His anticipation of being in Amara's presence was wreaking havoc with his nervous system.

Prior to the beginning of the business day, Amara and Mrs. Rogers had put the finishing touches on the small amphitheater where the meeting was scheduled to take place. Easels were strategically placed, projectors were working, podium mikes were on; all was well, but for the life of her Amara could not stop her stomach from quivering. She knew it was because of Keino. He was in her and around her; his invisible cloak covered her day and night. Keino had passed through the office several times over the last few weeks but today would be the day her team presented findings of the last month of assessments and evaluations. The thought of presenting formally with Keino present sent an energy through her over which she had no control. Her team was ready, all extremely professional and experts at their assigned tasks. It was all done. Lights, cameras, action—this was her show.

Amara had dressed to be seen. She not only wanted Keino to be impressed with her ability to pull together the massive components of his staff; she was clear that she wanted him to see her as a woman.

She wore a red silk suit with a straight skirt ending just below the knee. A red lace camisole under a double-breasted form-fitting jacket. The outfit was accessorized with bold Senegalese gold jewelry at her neck and on her ears. On her wrist she wore a slender gold Piaget watch. Sheer, off black hose encased the legs Keino found so enticing and she wore three-inch, black leather heels.

As she entered the room Keino's eyes followed her. She could feel his eyes on her. He was so taken by the way she moved. The undulation of her hips sent him almost over the edge. He was grateful for his years of discipline and self-control. They had not been alone together since the night they first met, but, at that moment she could feel the warmth of his desire travel down her back as her peripheral vision took in the sight of him. Whenever they were in the same room they were both well aware of the smoldering heat just beneath the surface, and they were clear that it would not take much to ignite a full blown flame. They had both decided, without informing the other, to play with the fire, in spite of doubts and preconceived notions. When the presentation was finished, Keino was once again impressed with Amara's ability to synthesize information. The assembled staff of Mazrui Industries seemed equally impressed. As she presented, there was rapt attention, some laughter when appropriate, and genuine respect for the work that had been done. Amara praised the staff highly and highlighted many of the outstanding attributes of individual staff members.

The manual was well received. The comments were, that it was user friendly and therefore easily implemented.

Keino and Amara, consummate professionals, kept their respective composures as the day wore on, but underneath their in-control exteriors, were two very tense, sexually charged individuals. At this point neither could deny that there was a raging attraction. What they didn't know was how they would appease their respective hungers.

At the close of the day, with congratulatory remarks and good-byes, Keino approached Amara. He wanted to touch her, to stroke her silken sleeve knowing it could not compare to her bare flesh. Instead he said, "Amara, that was extremely well done. Your staff was able to pull together the process to get us back on track. Thanks to you, we are now ready to move ahead with our expansion."

With as much control as she could summon, Amara responded, "Thank you, Keino, you have a great group of people. They were very open and therefore easy to work with."

As Keino and Amara exchanged pleasantries, what they really wanted was to touch each other, to quench the thirst they were both feeling. They wanted desperately to share a special look or touch meant only for them—instead, they allowed a warm smile and a professional handshake to suffice. As Amara turned to leave, Keino said with quiet authority, "I hope to see you at the company gathering this evening."

Amara answered, with a slight tremor in her voice, "Yes, my entire family plans to attend." Breathing deeply and forcing herself to remain in control of her emotions she continued. "It was such a great idea to have a company like Mazrui Industries host a banquet honoring community leaders. I am sure it will inspire a lot of community work, with people every year vying for recognition."

The underlying sensuality in his voice always captivated her; this time was no exception as he said, "That's the idea. There is so much work to be done to improve the plight of our people around the world. My parents never allow us to become a part of a community without giving back."

In her wonderful, low soft voice, Amara said, "Sounds like we have the same parents."

Keino threw back his head and laughed in his rich warm way. "I look forward to meeting your parents tonight, please introduce me."

Feeling as though she were melting, Amara said, "I will, I am sure they will enjoy meeting you."

Keino satisfied his need to touch Amara by lifting his hand and gently stroking her shoulder as he said, "Thank you again." Then, as he turned to go he said, "Until tonight."

As he walked away, Amara watched him leave. His gait propelled by strong muscular legs was elegant, his stride was indeed befitting royalty. She knew she wanted to belong to this man. A part of her felt so lost because she had never felt this way before. No man had ever elicited the idea of throwing caution to the wind, let alone actually doing it. But she knew that if she felt as safe, as secure and as magnetized as she did now, if he ever touched her in the way that a man touches a woman he desires, she would burn like molten lava. Oh, how she wanted to burn in his arms. She couldn't believe herself. This was so very new. She had begun to believe this kind of attraction just wasn't in the cards for her; Keino Mazrui, the African Adonis himself, had made her rethink her position. But one thing she could not rethink—he was a continental African and that brought with it a whole new set of rules. A deep sigh was all she could manage as she packed her case to head for home.

On her way home, Amara decided to make a detour. Seven years prior her father had established the nonprofit organization called Mentoring The Boys, fondly known as MTB. The organization was formed to give guidance, educationally and emotionally, to needy boys between the ages of seven and seventeen. Two years prior the board of directors under Dr. James Terrell's masterful orchestration had purchased and refurbished a former warehouse space in a newly renovated section of the city and built a state-of-the-art facility. The building was chosen because of its accessibility to bus lines and freeways and therefore attracted boys from all over the city. MTB opened at seven A.M. and closed at ten P.M. six days a week. A highly trained staff of teachers, psychologists, nurses, and administrative personnel were scheduled into the program on a daily basis. The square footage of the building allowed for a well equipped library, separate classroom space, a gymnasium, and a cafeteria where youngsters were fed without charge. A variety of delectable snacks were also available for adults to purchase. Amara and her sisters volunteered their services usually on Saturday mornings, but today she had a need just to stop by and get the shot of adrenaline she always received when she thought about, and immersed herself in the magical work that was her father's brainchild. As she turned onto the street where MTB was located she marveled at how the new coats of paint and the revived architecture in the neighborhood mimicked the restoration of the lives of many of the boys who walked through the doors of MTB. She parked her car in the rear of the building in a parking lot designed with ample space to fit the facility's needs. As she opened the door and walked leisurely into the building, she smiled as the warmth of the colors and the infusion of light into the space from a bank of floor to ceiling windows soothed and calmed her spirit. As she continued with a light stride toward the administrative offices she heard an exuberant shout.

"Ms. Amara, Ms. Amara."

She turned in the direction of the voice and saw waving in her direction with a big smile on his face, Bobby Hollis. Bobby was a thirteen-year-old mentee whose face was so open, bright, and magnetic that whenever she saw him he melted Amara's heart. She tilted her head, smiled, placed both hands on her hips and said with the pleasure of seeing him not at all concealed in her voice, "Little Mr. Man, what are you doing out here roaming the halls instead of doing some work?"

With bubbling joy and laughter laced in his response, Bobby said, "Ah, Ms. Amara, see, I saw you when you walked in the building, and I just had to tell you, that friend of yours that you talked to gave me a job.

"Every Saturday afternoon I have to bathe, feed, and walk her two dogs and I get a nice piece of change, too. I just wanted to say thank you, Ms. Amara, thank you."

"Oh, Bobby, that's wonderful. Mrs. Albertson is not a friend of mine she is a client, but when she mentioned that she needed a young person to help with her dogs I just knew you would be the right person. Now make sure you do a good job for her."

"You know I will, Ms. Amara. You always tell me I'm not just representing myself but I'm representing my mom, you, and MTB. I have to do well."

Bobby and Amara wrapped each other in a warm embrace. Amara gave Bobby a final pat on the back and he went bouncing off down the hall in the direction of the cafeteria. As she walked away Amara couldn't help but play back in her head Bobby's words about who he was representing. A deep sadness enveloped her as she replayed the absence of the mention of a father. A loss for Bobby for sure, but she was certain not to have Bobby in his life was a greater loss for his father, wherever he was. Amara entered the administrative offices where she encountered smiles and an occasional "Hello, Ms. Terrell."

She spotted Margie Payne, the office manager, walking toward her. "Hi, Margie."

"Hi, yourself," Margie replied in her usual warm, homey manner. "What on earth are you doing here this late on a weekday?"

Amara kept walking toward the volunteers office as she said, "Would you believe me if I told you

I was just in the neighborhood so I thought I would just drop by?" They both laughed thinking of the lack of truth in Amara's response. "No, really I came by because there is a list of potential contributors Dad asked me to get a copy of so that we can start our annual fund-raising campaign. Do you know where he might have left it?'

"Yes, ma'am, I do. I'll get it for you."

While waiting for Margie to return, Amara conversed with other office personnel. She caught up on the latest statistics of children's births, marriages, graduations, college entrances, and looked at a few photographs and o–o'ed and ah–ah'ed over beautiful children and handsome significant others. Margie returned.

"Here you are, Amara. See you Saturday."

"I'll be here"

With an added spring in her step, Amara headed for home.

Chapter 9

As Amara entered the door of her home, her telephone was ringing. She dropped her attaché near the front door and picked up her cordless telephone from the table in the foyer. She walked to her ecru colored sofa, sat down and pushed talk. Immediately she heard, "All right, Amara, get it together. You are late already. You should have been home an hour ago. We are all meeting at Mom and Dad's. I've hired a limo so that we can all ride in comfort and not concern ourselves with cars and driving. See you in one hour."

"Hello to you, too, Adana, I'll be on time. Love you." She smiled, and hung up. Adana, that sister was going to organize the world. The family could always count on her to keep their itinerary straight whether they wanted her to or not. She was born to be a lawyer. She could make a case out of anything.

Amara walked over to the cherry wood hall table and placed the telephone in its cradle. She picked up her briefcase from its resting place near the door and walked through the peach and cream colored living room, making her way upstairs to the bedroom to bathe and change for the evening's festivities. Amara's home epitomized comfort and beauty. Along with cherry wood and mahogany accents used as her home's accessories, her walls were adorned with her favorite Charles Bibb and Romare Bearden paintings. African masks and statues strategically and elegantly took their places on walls and in corners. Beauty and harmony were her signature style.

She entered the spacious master suite and began to run a fragrant tub filled with lavender and jasmine oils. She pushed the stereo remote and filled her home with the sounds of her favorite jazz trio. As she prepared to join her family at the Mazrui company event, her thoughts, as though on auto pilot, strayed to Keino. As she undressed and stepped into her tub, her body relived the touch of his hands, the sound of his voice, and his sensual stare. Her traitorous feelings were making it abundantly clear that she was in over her head. Here he was, a man who personified everything she did not want; a power broker, driven, probably conceited, probably had no room for another person in his life, and she wanted him so much she could feel him all over her. As she speculated about what Keino might be like, in the deep recesses of his soul, she had to admit grudgingly that what she really knew about the inner workings of his mind was nothing. What she did know was that he was magnetic, powerful, seductive and that he made her weak with just a glance.

The Terrell family entered the Westchester Hotel's Grand Ballroom. The Terrell women were stunning, each in a full length gown befitting her stature and style. James was the picture of sophistication in black formal wear. He was indeed proud as he escorted his family through the ballroom doors. As they entered, Ana and James saw a number of colleagues and friends. Both had long-standing ties to community endeavors, social and charitable.

As her parents renewed old acquaintances and her sisters chatted with friends and each other, Amara scanned the room hoping for a glimpse of the African god himself, Mr. Keino Mazrui. As she perused the room she saw him across the floor in the midst of a group of people, two of whom resembled him in very different ways. He had the woman's eyes, nose, and hair texture. He had the man's coloring, height, build and a more refined version of his regal posture. She surmised these had to be his parents. She had heard rumors around the office before she left that they were expected to fly in from Kenya to assist their son in hosting this gala event.

Keino was even more handsome in formal attire. Looking at him was torturously sublime. As she continued to survey the group she noticed an exquisite young woman standing arm in arm with Keino. Much too chummy to be a sister, she thought to herself, and besides, she knew Keino had no sisters and his brothers' wives, she was certain, would not be that proprietary in their affections. The woman was beautiful. She stood about five feet ten inches, willowy slender body, deep cocoa rich skin, long elegant neck, closely cropped au naturelle hair, wide, expressive, almond shaped eyes, and a bearing which attested to excellent breeding. As the cocoa beauty leaned to whisper in Keino's ear, he looked up straight into Amara's eyes. Amara smiled and turned to walk away and Keino's heart sank at what he knew she thought, seeing the lovely Makena on his arm. At that moment he knew he had to clear up his personal matters and move on with his life, and he knew Amara was the one with whom he wanted to spend his time for however long. Makena had flown in with his parents to surprise him, and that she had. She was accustomed to having her way and getting what she wanted. She wanted Keino. When they were betrothed as children it had meant little to her, but as they got older and his reputation as a man of quality and means grew, so did her ardor for him. She was certain he was the kind of husband she deserved. As guests continued socializing, bells rang as a signal for everyone to find their tables and be seated for dinner. Keino, seated at the head table, surveyed the room to find Amara. He hoped that she would remember to find him after the festivities to introduce her family. If not, he would find her. He was determined that she not be allowed to remove herself from him because of a misperception. Amara sat at a table not far from the head table. He had arranged the seating so that in his own way he would be near her.

She and her family were seated with Mary Rogers and three other Mazrui managers. They all shared pleasant conversation over elegant food and fine wines. Mrs. Rogers was the only one at the table who had known Keino since he was a young man, and she shared very touching stories about his generosity and his compassionate spirit. Her stories touched Amara and convinced her even further that she had misjudged Keino. It didn't matter now, he appeared to be very taken. She should have known.

Near the middle of the meal the program began. The Mazrui men spoke, lauding everyone for their attendance and for the civic minded leadership shown by so many. Awards were given, and to the delight and surprise of the Terrell family, Dr. James Terrell was a recipient for his work with the organization he'd founded called MTB—Mentoring The Boys.

His daughters stood as his name was called. Their mother cried tears of joy. She knew of the behind the scenes love and dedication her husband had put into his organization and she knew him to be so very deserving of this award. This not only provided a plaque in his honor, but funds to carry the entire organization for one year. Ana had been told in advance, and it had been difficult keeping this secret from her husband and daughters, but tonight made it all worthwhile.

At the end of the evening as those in attendance quietly chatted and offered congratulations to those who received awards, Keino spotted the Terrells, and while Makena was otherwise occupied, with purposeful strides he entered the Terrell family circle, his eyes never leaving Amara. The form-fitting strapless white and gold gown she wore left him breathless and desiring her more than ever. As he entered the group, he said, "Dr. Terrell, I would once again like to congratulate you on your work outside of the university." Once again his eyes met Amara's. He said, "Your daughter Amara has already spoken so highly of you I wanted to be sure to extend my congratulations in a less formal way."

As Keino was waxing eloquently about James Terrell's work, his eyes always managed to find Amara.

Cassandra whispered discreetly to her sister Afiya.

"Do you see the way he's looking at Amara or is it just me?"

"No, it's not you, it's them. We need to talk to sister girl."

As Keino finished his sentence he asked, "Which daughter is the interior designer?"

"I am guilty." Cassandra smiled.

Keino stated, "Mrs. Rogers did get your message to me and I look forward to a consultation soon."

"Great," said Cassandra, "I look forward to working with you."

As Keino was about to bid his farewell, Ana Terrell said, "Mr. Mazrui."

He responded, "Keino, please."

"When your mother was introduced earlier this evening something about her was so familiar. Is she Ethiopian?"

"Why, yes. I would love for you to meet her. If you will wait a moment longer I will ask my mother to join us."

As Keino left the group to locate his mother and bring her back to introduce her to the Terrells, Amara and her sisters watched Keino's distinctive stride as he moved confidently across the room. As Keino's figure faded into the crowd the three sisters turned toward Amara, encircling her, and began an inquisition in tones their preoccupied parents could not hear.

Afiya was first. She looked directly at her sister and in slow, fluid speech said, "M—y m—y, Amara, I can see why Mr. Magic had you all in a tizzy. And I saw the way he was looking at you. Did you feel it? I know you felt it because I felt it."

Cassandra was next. With arms folded and an index finger tapping a forearm, she agreed. "Yes, indeed, I think we all felt it. Just look at him. I'd say not only is he fine, but the way he looked at you, you look as good to him as buttered bread does to a hungry man."

Adana, always the practical one, added, "I'm certain his good looks are made even better by his financial holdings."

Afiya interjected, "Looks to me like what he wants to hold is Amara."

At that point, no one could contain the laughter that spilled over. By this time Amara was both embarrassed and amused. Seeing Keino starting to head in their direction she said in a stage whisper, "Stop! You people need to stop jumping to conclusions. We don't really even know the man. All he has been to me is gracious, kind, and a perfect gentleman. Now stop and pull yourselves together before he comes back."

Keino returned, walking arm in arm with his mother. She was such a warm, elegant lady and so very pretty with youthful looks that belied her age.

Ana stepped forward. "Mrs. Mazrui," she said, "I am so happy to meet you. It was a wonderful event."

Ana Terrell introduced her family. When she came to Amara, Keino's mom said, "Such beautiful daughters and this one has my sister's name."

"Is that so?" said Ana. "It is odd that you should say that. I named Amara after my college roommate at Spelman."

They all stopped when Adina Mazrui said, "My sister went to Spelman and my sister's name is Amara."

"Could this be true?" cried Ana. "Was your maiden name Zagwe?"

"Yes, and my sister, of course, was Amara Zagwe. Oh, my God."

They grabbed each other and held on tightly, asking question after question, crying and laughing simultaneously. The others looked on happily, astounded.

Keino said, looking straight at Amara, "I knew it was a special name."

At the moment they were embracing with their eyes, Makena and Judge Mazrui walked up. Judge Mazrui walked over to hear his wife fill him in on the great find of the evening. Makena simply stared at the lovely young woman whose name had prompted all of the commotion. It also was not lost on her the way in which Keino embraced this woman without touching her. Makena sneered to herself. *These American women, what is the draw for African men?*

At that moment, Judge Mazrui said, "In all of the excitement we forgot to introduce our family friend, Makena Rono, perhaps one day our daughter." He looked pointedly at Keino. At the moment the judge looked at Keino, the sisters cringed in unison feeling at once sadness and disappointment for Amara. Amara's heart sank. She felt a tremendous loss. What she had lost she was not sure. Keino smiled a strained smile, knowing clearly he had to disappoint his father and incur the wrath of Makena's family. But for time with Amara he was willing to withstand it all.

Chapter 10

Amara prepared for bed, slowly undressing, replaying in her head the evening's events. As proud as she was of her father; and as grateful as she was for the accolades paid him, a deep sadness enveloped her. She couldn't shake the feeling she had remembering Judge Mazrui's introduction of the beautiful young woman who had accompanied the Mazrui family to the awards banquet. Amara felt as though a hole had been hollowed out inside of her. She had no idea how deeply she had fallen for Keino until that introduction. She could feel hot tears burning the backs of her eyes as she thought about the possessive way in which Ms. Makena Rono had held onto Keino.

Amara felt so ridiculous. This man had not even expressed a real interest in her. Yes, she could sense something when they were together but that could just be imaginative longings on her part; besides, the last thing she wanted was a relationship with a domineering, culturally insensitive man. Who was she kidding? The Keino she felt she knew couldn't be any of those things, and because she wanted him, she was willing to take a chance to see who he really was. Now she would never have that chance. He was quite occupied.

As Amara reached over to turn off the lamp beside her bed her telephone rang. She looked at her clock, it registered twelve forty-five A.M. Which sister was this? she thought, smiling through her tears. Whichever sister it was would be a pleasant reprieve from her sad thoughts. The minute she picked up the receiver she felt him; her breathing became erratic as she voiced a tentative, sultry, "Hello."

The velvety seductive tone with which she was now so familiar began, "Amara, please forgive the lateness of the hour. It is not my habit to be rude, but there are a few things I would like to discuss with you."

The first thing that leaped to Amara's mind was the project. Her questions rushed out on one breath of air. "Keino, what's wrong? Did something go wrong with the project? What happened?"

Keino had been so preoccupied with clearing up the Makena calamity, that it had not occurred to him that his call would alarm Amara and have her focusing on work. He rushed to put her at ease. "Please, do not be alarmed. This conversation has nothing to do with Mazrui Industries. I am a very direct man, Amara. Some say arrogant, and insensitive. I am neither of those things. What I am is a man who is very clear about his path and his obligations. I am not generally open to allowing anything or anyone to cause me to stray from my path or interfere with fulfilling my obligations. You, Amara Terrell, are presenting a problem for me."

Shock made her body stiffen. Words were lost in her throat. Her mind struggled to pull together what she had heard. Did he say she was a problem? She could feel her temper start to slowly smolder. "Excuse me, Mr. Mazrui, did you say that I am a problem?"

Her response annoyed him, but in some peculiar way he found humor in their exchange. "I can see that I have offended you. That was not my intention. Diplomacy is not my gift. By the way, my name is still Keino. It slides so beautifully from your lips, I'd hate to give up the privilege of hearing it from time to time."

Now, she didn't know whether to hang up on him, or allow her curiosity to get the better of her and listen to what he had to say. She decided to take the latter course. "Keino," she asked with exasperation in her tone, "why did you call?"

"I called," he said with a kind of intensity she had not heard before, "because I have developed a hunger for you I want to explore. The things I experience when I am around you are new, uncharted territory for me, Amara. There is a reason for this magnetic pull—I must know what it is. There are also some misconceptions about me that I must clear up tonight. I saw your face when Makena was introduced. You must understand that I am not a man who can contemplate getting to know one woman if I am emotionally committed to another. Shall I send a car for you?"

A shiver streaked through her. Amara was frozen; he was right, diplomacy was not his gift, but honesty certainly was. She had no intention of seeing him tonight. This encounter with him had left her more befuddled than ever. Tonight, she needed to be away from him to clear her head—to process what he had shared. And so she answered, "Keino, I want us to talk, but not tonight. Can we have this conversation tomorrow in the light of day?"

"I am so sorry, Amara, I am flying out at six in the morning." There was silence and then he said, "I have an idea. Meet me in Curacao day after tomorrow. I will make all of the travel arrangements. I'll arrange for you to have a villa for the four days that we are there. Your private villa, no pressure. I want you near enough to spend time with me. My need for you, Amara, is very strong, but the choice is yours. We need to explore our options in a place where we are free to do so. Though I will be involved in a few meetings, I will send a car for you every day so that we might dine together and enjoy the nightly festivities. You can spend your days in the spa, exploring any new beauty treatments." With a contemplative smoothness he added, "Though I must admit, it is impossible for me to see how you could improve upon perfection. If it will entice you more, an expense account will be available to you for any amusements which strike your fancy. You will be my guest. In my home, it has always been customary that guests not want for anything. Amara, be my guest for four days and allow me to show you how much I welcome your presence."

She heard the deep commanding seduction in his voice and reacted physically. She could feel the heat radiate throughout the center of her body and spiral out through her extremities. In a voice glazed with desire, she asked, "Why should I go with you Keino?"

Keino, the master of persuasion continued. "I am serious about everything I do. It is not my way to toy with anything. I don't want to play with you,

Amara. I want to learn your ways, anticipate your moods. I want you in a way that I have never wanted anyone. We need this time. Say you'll come."

When Keino finished, Amara was rendered speechless. With each word he uttered her blood had begun racing, her pulse thundering, her heart melting. She searched her brain for sanity; she found need and desire. She wanted Keino. She wanted to let him explain away her fears and her reservations. She wanted him to explain it all away because she wanted him. What was left of her rational self tried to buy time. She responded with as much calm as she could muster, "Keino, whatever we need to say or do we can say when you return. I can't just pick up and leave for four days. I have a company, it's not Mazrui Industries, but it is my company and I need to be here. I can't just leave."

Keino countered, "Yes, you can, Amara. I know your schedule, and four days will not damage your business. You have a very competent staff. Say yes, Amara, we need this time."

Amara, feeling herself being pulled into Keino's plan, started speaking rapidly. "How will it look, international playboy swoops provincial Virginia girl off her feet?"

Keino laughed; the velvet tones washed over Amara. "Amara, do you care what the world sees? The people that matter will understand. I'll send a car for you at noon in two days. That will give you time to put things in order. I will arrange for the company plane to transport you to Curacao. The attendant on the plane will have an itinerary for you. If I do not see you in Curacao I will know that this mysterious pull I am experiencing is merely an illusion and I will pursue it no further."

Through a fog of emotions, Amara heard herself say in very terse tones, "Mr. Keino Mazrui, I know you have little regard for the workings of my life, but I do have a life and I am not, at this stage in it, going to drop everything and run off with you to satisfy your need to talk. You may talk to me. I don't mind talking, but it will be when it is convenient for us both, and by the way, it will be here in good ole Virginia. Good night."

As Amara took a deep breath and settled back on her pillow, Keino was left holding a telephone receiver which was transmitting the annoying sound of a dial tone. In a flash, Keino's mood went from fiery indignation to agonized amazement. He looked at the phone as though it had grown a head, and with a startled expression on his face uttered, "No woman has ever refused a request from me, taken me to task and hung up on me all in one fell swoop."

As he got up from his chair to make his way to his bedroom to prepare for his early morning departure, he found himself laughing loudly in disbelief. Amara Terrell had actually dismissed him. There was a first time for everything. He spoke to the empty room, smiling all the while. "Oh, Ms. Amara Terrell, independent lioness, you have met your match. I will see you soon."

He slept with visions of the feisty beauty dancing through his head.

In the small hours of the morning the shrill ringing of the telephone shook Keino from a very pleasant sleep. His slumber had been filled with erotic dreams of the honey-colored vixen he knew as Amara. The ringing telephone jolted him again. He reached over, and with eyes closed answered with a gruff, "Hello."

The intense tenor voice of his longtime business associate Bradford Donald replied, "Keino, hey man, this is Brad. I know it's the middle of the night, but I needed to stop you before you headed out to meet me in Curacao in the morning. Things are in an uproar here. There are several things I need to get straight before our meeting. Our development plans are stalled if I can't get the clearances I need. I thought it was all handled, that everything was a go until an hour ago when Watts had a message delivered that he has changed his mind about selling the one piece of land we need to complete the project. I could kill him but"—he laughed—"I'm not sure that would get me the land, and I'd have a jail sentence to face. Man, I'll get back to you when we can move forward."

Keino, fully awake now, rushed to reassure his friend and associate. "Hold on, Brad, not so fast. What can I do to help rectify the situation? This sounds to me like your personal life has put a crimp in your business dealings. If I remember correctly, this same Henry Watts was once upon a time going to be your father-in-law. Surely you can put your pride aside and either talk to Henry or call Justine, your ex fiancée, and have her intervene on your behalf. What is it worth to you, man? Is your pride more important than the project?"

The silence on the other end of the line let Keino know that he had hit a sensitive nerve. Bradford Donald was a man from humble beginnings who had fought his way through the corporate world to make a niche for himself as a land developer. He and Keino had met one summer during a college exchange program at the London School of Economics. They had become fast friends, recognizing in each other a tenacity, forthrightness, and loyalty not common among the masses. The two of them, Bradford, an imposing ex-football player with pecan-colored skin and a broad smile that displayed perfectly strong, white teeth, and the handsome Keino Mazrui caused heads to turn wherever they went. Their friendship had stood the test of time and each trusted the other with his life. In dry slow tones Bradford Donald responded, "Man if I didn't love you like a brother, I'd put a hit man out on you and Henry Watts. Okay, so you got me on that one. I'll still get back to you."

With that, Bradford Donald hung up. Keino looked at the phone, smiled, and asked, "Is this my night to have the telephone slammed in my face?"

He punched his pillows to get the desired level of comfort, stretched his legs, closed his eyes, and prayed that he could return to visions of Amara in his dreams.

Chapter 11

Saturday morning arrived not at all too soon for Amara. This was a weekend that she was very much looking forward to. She could erase thoughts of Keino from her mind and indulge in many of her favorite pastimes. She had scheduled two hours at her health club for a workout with her trainer, and a massage. One hour at the mentoring program where she volunteered, and an afternoon with her childhood friend Veronica Strong for antiquing and lunch. The evening would be spent at a concert with Robert King, a family friend for whom she felt no chemistry, but whose company she enjoyed. He was much like the brother she had never had. Though Amara arrived at the health club early to meet her trainer, it appeared that a number of other people had the same desire to be early. The club was teeming with active bodies in varying stages of fitness, grunting, groaning, and perspiring all done to piped in music and a number of soundless television sets hanging from the ceiling. The television sets hung in plain view of souls torturing themselves in the name of fitness and health.

Frederick, Amara's trainer, a very young, very Nordic-looking man came through the door a short time after she did. He spotted her as she sat reading a book. He walked up to her, tapped her on the shoulder and said, "Hi, Amara. I'm here, let's get to it."

Mr. No-nonsense himself Amara thought. "Well, Frederick, I'm as ready as I'll ever be. You know this is not my favorite thing to do. But I want my heart to stay in good shape and I want to be strong."

"Well stick with it, my lady, and strength and power will be yours, I promise you."

Amara moved toward the machines, bottled water and book in hand, to join the ranks of those grunting, groaning, and profusely perspiring.

After her workout and massage, Amara was so relaxed she felt as if she had to pour herself into her car for the ride to North Lee Street to meet Veronica for lunch and a round of antique hunting. Veronica was five feet five inches tall, shapely, articulate, smart and as sassy and as flirty as a woman can legally be. Her pixie haircut, wide eyes, and translucent sable skin caused her to turn many heads. As Amara drove she engaged the speaker to her cellular telephone. She pressed the number six, which was her code for Veronica's telephone number. After two rings she heard her friend's deep, mellow, sexy tones echo, "You've reached Veronica Strong; it's your money, start talking."

Amara responded with feigned annoyance "Veronica, stop answering your telephone like that." With barely controlled laughter, she continued. "Suppose I was a very desirable man wanting to meet you, and you came on sounding like Ms. Flip Sassy Mouth. What would he think?"

The quick-witted Veronica answered, "He'd better think, let me hurry up and get to that sweet sassy woman. If he can't think like that, I don't want him."

"Veronica, there is no hope for you. If you weren't my friend I'd just give up."

With feigned contriteness, Veronica's retort was, "I know, I know. At least you know I mean well."

"Yes, I know you do. I'll meet you in ten minutes."

A little more than ten minutes later, Veronica and Amara found themselves between Cameron and Queen Streets in a building known as Old Town Market and Antique Mall. They browsed together and separately, each enjoying just looking and sharing their fond appreciation of the old. From the time they were little girls until they were well into their teens, Veronica's paternal grandmother, a schoolteacher whose name was Samantha Strong had been an avid antique collector. She had taken Amara and Veronica on many hunts for antiques at a bargain. Before she passed away she had managed to share her knowledge and love of antiques with both of them. Neither of them ever lost the love of antiquing. Amara's pleasure was found in looking for antique silver, and antique furnishings. Veronica had developed a fondness for antique glass. In spite of her sometimes flip attitude, when antiquing Veronica became the quintessential CPA. As the owner of a small accounting firm, in her serious moments it was clear to everyone that she was a professional accountant.

"Amara, come over here, I think I've found something."

Amara turned her head to see her friend fingering a green maple leaf water pitcher with gold trim. Amara put down the silver antique picture frame she was holding and walked in Veronica's direction.

"What did you find?"

"Look at this," she said in a slight stage whisper. "I think this pitcher is an authentic Page." Veronica knew the name Page was synonymous with quality. "Aside from being beautiful it would be a fantastic investment."

"Wow, it is beautiful. I think you should get it. It would really add to your collection."

"I think you're right, but you know Grammy Sam would walk out of heaven if I didn't haggle the way she taught us. You know what she always said."

They both repeated in unison with wide smiles on their faces, "Never pay the asking price without trying to get away with less."

As Veronica headed off to discuss her idea of a bargain price with the store clerk, Amara called after her in joking banter. "Your grandmother must have been a West African market woman in another life."

They both laughed at the accuracy of that image. Thirty minutes later Amara and Veronica were leaving the antiques store happy as larks, because Veronica had accomplished a bloodless coup by wearing down the shopkeeper until he relented and agreed to a twenty percent discount. Amara had thoroughly enjoyed watching Veronica overwhelm the store owner acting as clerk, with facts, figures, and charm. They walked down the street headed toward one of their favorite sandwich and salad eateries. The exuberant Veronica threw her head back, her hands into the air and yelled, "Yes!"

Her laughter was contagious as Amara said, "You did it again, girlfriend, you did it again. Let's go eat."

Veronica announced, "Now I'm really hungry. Some of Angelo's fresh bread and seafood salad sure would be great right about now."

"For once, I agree with you." Laughed Amara.

The two left their cars parked and walked around the corner and up two blocks to their favorite sandwich shop. Angelo's was a small quiet restaurant with the feel of a European bistro. Amara and Veronica chose a table outside on the sunny patio. Though the day was cool, the sun shone brightly emanating enough warmth to make the outdoor patio very pleasant. When they were seated, and had placed their orders, Veronica almost shouted, "Hey, Amara, I almost forgot to ask you to give me an update on your latest client. We've both been so caught up I haven't had a chance to get the low-down. So, what's up?"

"Strange that you should ask," Amara said pensively. "Thoughts of my new client seem to cross my mind continually. As a matter of fact, he called me last night after the banquet asking me to meet him in Curacao."

"Oh-oh, things are heating up fast," Veronica said excitedly. "When are you leaving?"

"I am not leaving," was Amara's impatient retort.

"What?" said Veronica in disbelief. "Pray tell, why not?"

"Because I am not going to jump up and run off with a man I don't even know, disrupt my schedule and my life just because he says"—now she imitated Keino's accent as she said—"Fly away with me, I need to talk to you."

Veronica broke into unbridled laughter listening to Amara's best Keino imitation. "Amara, you are too much. So, what are you going to do?"

Amara answered, while habitually combing her hair with her fingers, "I don't know what I'm going to do. I do know that before I go rushing off anywhere with Mr. Wonderful I will have spent a lot more time with him right here in Virginia."

With a hint of teasing Veronica asked, "Seriously, Amara, what do you really think about the man?"

A slow easy smile began on Amara's lips and rested in her eyes as she said, "I think he is one of the most beautiful creatures God ever fashioned. He is brilliant, and he is probably used to having anybody and anything that he wants." At that moment, the smile shifted and determination showed on her face. "I'm not going to lie down and whimper that easily. I don't know if I can trust him any farther than I can see him. As I told my sisters, this is an African man, a continental African man. African royalty, no less. These are uncharted waters for me."

She tilted her head to one side and with a gleam in her eyes said, "But I must remind myself that if the truth be known, I am African American royalty. I come from a long line of brassy, brilliant, sassy, scintillating, strong, self-possessed sisters and I'm going to give Mr. Keino Mazrui a run for his money."

Veronica looked at Amara, smiled and said, "I hope he's ready."

The two friends finished their lunches and said their good-byes. Veronica headed home and Amara set off in the direction of the mentoring center for her Saturday volunteering stint.

Chapter 12

In the cool of the evening, Robert King, tall, rawboned, bearded, with an appealing nut-brown face, stood motionless at Amara's front door. Once again he had elected to inflict upon himself the pleasure, and the pain, of accompanying Amara to an event, to serve as her escort. To her, he was a friend, a longtime family friend. For Amara he was as comfortable as a worn chenille robe accompanied by lush warm slippers. He, on the other hand, had loved her from the moment he'd met her, but he knew the feeling had never been reciprocated. Tonight would be no different.

"Why do I put myself through this," he muttered to himself. "You'd think by now, Professor, your lessons would have been learned. Well, the truth is, I'd rather be with Amara as a friend than no Amara at all. And so it is, and so it is." He stretched out his long arm, which had been held at his side, and extended a long slender finger, pushed Amara's doorbell, and awaited a response.

Amara heard the doorbell and rushed to put the finishing touches on her face. Though her day had been full, thoughts of Keino had managed to creep into the deep recesses of her soul. She whispered to herself, "All right, Amara, the African Adonis is not going to take over your every waking thought, you are going to go on with your life and let Mr. Keino Mazrui go on with his. Robert is here, and you are going to go out and enjoy the warm companionship of a dear friend. Who needs fireworks?" At that moment she could hear her friend Veronica's voice in her mind say, *You do, Amara! You need the fireworks and everything that comes with them.*

Amara smiled to herself and said aloud jokingly to no one in particular while walking to answer the door, "Keino and Veronica are going to drive me crazy."

When she opened the door and saw the clean-cut well-dressed Professor Robert King standing there, though she felt no fireworks she felt safe and serene. "Hello, Robert, sorry it took a minute, final touches you know."

"Amara, you never need a final touch." Robert continued in as lighthearted a tone as he could produce. "Didn't you know that your perfection is legendary?"

Oblivious to Robert's feelings for her, Amara answered, gently laughing, "See, Robert, that's what friends are for. To tell those wonderful gracious lies."

Robert laughed with her, expressing a humor he did not feel. His retort was, "That's us, Amara, friends forever. Now, let's go watch the Alvin Ailey dancers leap for joy."

Robert placed his hand on Amara's shoulder

and fought the urge to kiss her by hurriedly moving her toward the door with a feigned concern about being late.

Once enclosed inside Robert's roomy sedan, Amara momentarily drifted into thoughts of Keino. She heard the sensuous caress of Keino's velvet tones whisper *Come with me to Curacao. Come with me, come.*

Her reverie was interrupted by Robert's playfully spoken, "A penny for your thoughts, my lady."

Shaking her head gently as if to remove cobwebs and bring herself back to earth, Amara responded, "Oh, my God, Robert, I'm sorry. I guess I floated away for a moment."

While driving, Robert looked at her from the corner of one eye and said, "Bringing your work home, no doubt. You are one of the most conscientious people I know, Amara. That's why I am so pleased you consented to join me tonight. When I saw the ad for the Ailey dancers I immediately thought of you. I knew it would lift your spirits. I know how you love live dance theater."

Amara folded her arms, nestled herself in the comfort of the seat cushions, tilted her head back on the headrest, and answered dreamily, "Thank you, Robert. I do love dance, and Ailey productions send me into a world of my own. The set design, the choreography, the costuming. The magic of it sweeps me away every time I see it. I really appreciate your thoughtfulness."

With unexpected intensity Robert said, "Amara, you know that your wishes are always my command."

The seriousness with which Robert spoke rushed up Amara's spine, with an uneasiness she had never felt before when with him. Plastering a smile on her face she said simply, "Thank you, Robert."

Keino Mazrui sat massaging his temples, warding off a headache which was proving to be a tremendous adversary to his willpower. Just as he took a cleansing breath, Mrs. Rogers walked over, touched him gently on the shoulder and said, "Mr. Mazrui, if you'd like a little less solitude you can join the rest of us. You made sure we have plenty of room."

Keino looked up and smiled warmly into an equally friendly gaze and said, "Thank you, Mrs. Rogers, but when I move again it will be to leave the theater. I am quite comfortable, thank you. Tell everyone to enjoy themselves."

"I will. Have a good evening."

After Mrs. Rogers made her exit Keino settled in his seat, breathing a sigh of relief that the throbbing in his head had decided to subside. As he turned to his left to take in the grandeur of the architecture of the theater in which he sat, he squinted, then blinked, wondering if his eyes were deceiving him. He stared frozen in place as the vision of loveliness, whom he had just the night before seen floating through his dreams, walked into the row below where he was seated. She did not see him but his view of her was perfect. Until that instant Keino had never been more grateful that he had honored his commitment to his newfound community by his patronage of the arts. He truly believed in Divine providence. There she was, Amara Terrell. Since he had not had to go to Curacao he had talked himself into joining his executive team for dinner and a performance of the Alivn Ailey dancers. How fortunate that the ancestors should place Amara in his path again. There she was, clad in a bronze-colored, V-necked wrap dress. The dress, which was nearly the color of her skin, was accentuated with a gold neckpiece and gold earrings. The man by her side was extremely attentive, causing Keino to react viscerally. He had never before been jealous of another man's attentions to a woman. But now he found himself consciously controlling his urge to walk over to the man in question and say, *Do not ever again touch my woman.* He almost laughed out loud at himself. Here he was, whipping himself up into a jealous rage over a woman who had hung up on him and had the distinct privilege of being the only woman in the world ever to have refused an invitation extended by him.

Robert and Amara sat down just as the house lights were dimmed. Amara could feel her breath still as she awaited the rise of the curtain. She loved all theater but dance was perhaps her favorite. As the performance began she sat mesmerized.

Keino sat, his gaze frozen on Amara. He watched her transport herself mentally onto the stage. He became one with her breath as he lowered his eyes to the space between her breasts and followed the rhythm of her beating heart with his own.

The intermission was short, the house lights remained dimmed, and Keino remained seated. Amara excused herself to go to the ladies' room and returned just as the curtain was to rise for the final time. Keino enjoyed the opportunity to watch her move without knowing that she was being observed. Everything about her excited him—her dancer's stride, the tilt of her head, her beauty, her intelligence. For him, she was magic. He could wait. He wanted time with her and time he would have, no matter who the fellow was who was sitting next to her.

When the final curtain call came Amara was emotionally spent. Amid the raucous applause and shouts of "Bravo," Keino left his seat and made his way to the place where he knew Amara and her date would have to exit. After he took his post at one of the front exit doors he found himself being thanked over and over again by members of his executive staff who had thoroughly enjoyed themselves. Just as he had finished shaking the last hand he saw Amara enter the theater lobby smiling and engrossed in conversation with the man he knew to be her escort. Just as Amara was ending an effusive hand gesture, explaining an observation of one of the pieces she had seen performed, she looked away from Robert into Keino's eyes. At first she thought she had gone mad or at best was having a temporary hallucination. Her mind was whirling. Wasn't Keino in Curacao? Why would he be here? Why would he be here now?

"Hello, Amara."

The voice was unmistakable, it really was Keino. Oh, God, it was! Why did he have to be so earth-shakingly gorgeous? His charcoal gray slacks, gray cashmere turtleneck and full-length, gray suede coat did not help to understate his virility. His garments hung on him like an adoring lover.

"Keino, what are you doing here? I mean, how are you?" Amara didn't recognize her own voice. It was a mixture of nervous confusion and uncontrolled excitement. Keino stepped forward so close that Amara could feel his breath. He took her hand and while gently holding it and looking directly into her eyes said, "I am here because business in Curacao was canceled and this performance has become a yearly outing for my executive staff. Tonight I decided to join them. Had I known you enjoyed dance I would have invited you." He paused and with a sly smile, continued, "And to answer your second question, I am doing very well, especially now."

At that moment Robert King, feeling as though he had become an eavesdropper listening in on a very private conversation, cleared his throat as a signal for someone to acknowledge his presence. Amara's head turned swiftly in Robert's direction as she pulled her hand from Keino's seductive grasp. With contrition ringing in her voice, Amara spoke. "I'm so sorry. Robert King, this is Keino Mazrui." She faced Robert, calmed herself and put on her best business face while saying, "Robert, Mr. Mazrui is my new client."

Keino and Robert both extended their hands for the traditional greeting. "I am very happy to meet you, Robert King."

Keino in size and manner threatened to overshadow Robert. Robert fought to hold his own. "I am always interested in meeting any of Amara's clients. Everything she does interests me."

The two men continued their verbal contest of wills, with Keino throwing the final barb. "I must say, I can truly understand your interest. It is not difficult for Amara to be the focus of anyone's attention. Until next week, Amara. Take care of her, Mr. Robert King. She is a treasure."

With all the grace and form befitting a king, Keino turned and walked away. Robert turned to Amara. "Well, you two seem chummy in a strangely combative sort of way. Is there something the rest of the world should be told about you two?"

Not wanting at that point to acknowledge anything about Keino, especially to Robert, Amara, with a tinge of frustration in her voice, downplayed Robert's remarks. "Robert, you are imagining things. Keino Mazrui is my newest client, no more, no less. Please let's get out of here. I really want to go home right now."

Robert responded calmly, not having believed a word of Amara's explanation. "As I said before, Amara, your wish is my command."

Chapter 13

Three weeks had come and gone since Keino's chance meeting with Amara. Both of them were moving ahead with their respective responsibilities, each always aware of feelings for the other, which were never far below the surface. Keino wrestled with what his next move should be since his customary directness was getting him nowhere. Amara was being tormented by her mixed feelings of relief that he seemed to have left her alone, and at the same time longing to see him in all of his uncompromising glory and to hear his mellow heart-melting tones.

Keino sat in his office. In spite of his harrowing schedule, thoughts of Amara stole their way into his day. He stretched one powerful long arm across his massive desk and dialed out on his private line. An exasperated Bradford Donald answered on the second ring.

"This is Brad Donald."

Keino, with a hint of amusement in his voice, responded in clipped perfect English overlaid with his East African accent. "Brad, this is Keino. I can tell by your tone there is a problem. Let's hear it."

Brad, relieved to hear his old friend's voice, unleashed all of his anguish. "Keino, man, this project is about to drive me to drink. If I have one more conference with Old Man Watts reneging on previously agreed upon verbal commitments, I promise you I won't be responsible for what I do."

Keino's voice was stern but sympathetic. "Yes, you would be responsible and because of that you are going to pull yourself together and charge back into battle with a strategy that will win the war. In this case, you know Watts's objections are obviously personal. You hold the cards of resolution. Swallow your pride and use them."

Bradford ground out his response between his teeth. "I am sick of Watts and his nonsense. I'm tired of his lowlife ways and his power plays. I'm sick of his name, his voice, and his ego. I swear, man, I'm going to punch that old man out. He is messing with my company revenue. Damn him!"

Keino, more forcefully this time, countered, "If you continue with this level of emotion, Watts will win. Remember, this man once upon a time was going to be your father-in-law. You were close. He treated you like a son. He is disappointed that you and Justine rearranged his life. Remember, you changed his plans also, not just yours. He's angry! You and Justine need to go to him together and work this through. What's the problem, man? Are you afraid of seeing Justine again?"

"Hey, man, Justine and I are cool. Her father can't get it through his thick skull that Justine and I ran our course and we are over and we are OK with that. Hell, she was the one who called it off."

"I'll say it again, Brad. The two of you, you and Justine, need to talk to her father."

The emotionally exhausted Bradford Donald replied, "Yeah, man, I know you're right. I've just got to get my head ready to put my hat in my hand and go talk to the old egomaniac." He took a breath. "Now, I know you didn't call me to hear all of this madness. What's happening in your world? What's up, Keino?"

The rich timbre of Keino's voice echoed throughout the room as he spoke freely to his friend about his company's current mergers and acquisitions. He filled him in on the lives of his brothers and his parents, all the while strategically turning over in his mind ways in which to bring up the subject of Amara Terrell, the lioness he hoped to tame. Bradford Donald detected an unusual awkwardness in Keino's voice as Keino said, "Brad, do you remember a conversation we had about a group of new consultants? One in particular, I mentioned to you some time ago? Her name is Amara Terrell."

"Yeah, yeah, man, I remember. I also remember saying that it sounded like you had the hots for Ms. Terrell. And I also remember saying I didn't see you foaming at the mouth over Makena like that. By the way, whatever happened with Ms. Terrell? Any hot dates to report?"

Keino's voice dropped in volume. "This is my problem, I invited her to Curacao and she refused." A tinge of exasperation laced his voice. "That was a first for me. I am not really clear where to step next. I need an African American perspective here. I might add, that though she refused my invitation I ran into her a few weeks ago at a concert and she was with an escort. I know she is not unattracted to me but it's as though she is running away from me. What's your take on the situation? By the way, I do not foam at the mouth over anyone."

After listening silently, Brad erupted in uncontrollable laughter. Hearing his laughter Keino responded with a humorous smirk in his voice. "I am so happy to be able to provide free entertainment to break up the monotony of your day."

Bradford Donald pressed on, relentlessly poking fun at his friend. "Man, I couldn't help it. Here you are, an international tycoon with more resources than you'll ever use in a lifetime, with women across the globe wanting to share your bed and your name, and some fine little sister from Virginia has your nose open and she doesn't even know it. Man, life is a trip." Brad's relaxed banter continued, "Look, Keino, first of all, this is not a business deal. Stop trying to steamroll your way into the woman's heart. Take your time. I am sure you came on too strong. Man, back up and woo the woman on her turf. Let her get comfortable with you. Dispel that myth that all African men want women barefoot and pregnant. That is a myth, isn't it, bro?"

It was Keino's turn to laugh. "Okay, Bradford, I owe you one."

"Naw, man, you owe me more than one. I need to make you come talk to Old Man Watts."

"Brad, I'll see you on the golf course Friday. I am going to shame you into submission."

"You can always try, brother, you can always try!"

With that the two friends hung up.

* * *

As the onyx colored sky fell on the close of another day, Amara sat in her home engrossed in the latest offerings of her favorite romance novelist. As she mentally raced with the heroine to the edge of what appeared to be a crucial dilemma, Amara's telephone began ringing. She reached for the receiver while continuing to read and in a voice overlaid with distance and distraction said, "Hello." She wasn't prepared for the response that came back to her.

"Hello, Amara, this is Keino. I hope I'm not disturbing you."

Amara jumped, initially startled by the sound of his voice. She dropped her book and began a furious attempt to compose herself. "Oh." She hesitated. "How are you, Keino? No, you're not disturbing me, I was just reading." With her heart still pounding she continued to take calming breaths as she waited for Keino to continue the conversation.

"From the sound of the distance in your voice when you answered the telephone, I would say the reading material was very intriguing."

Keino's ability to pick up on the slightest nuance in her behavior surprised her. "Actually, it's the latest work of one of my favorite romance writers. I must admit, the distraction is wonderful."

"Ah, the subject of romantic love—a Western phenomenon which has caused clearly as much pain as it has joy."

Moving gently into a quiet pensive tone, Amara stated, "Perhaps it has, but I would not want to live in a world without it."

"My dear Amara, your African ancestors lived for centuries with arranged marriages and no thought of romantic love as it is portrayed in the Western media, and I must say, they did very well."

Amara did not miss the stern, even way in which he spaced his words. "Keino, did you call to give me a lecture on the pros and cons of romantic love?"

Keino laughed. His silken tone became softer. "Perhaps one day, Amara, I will be able to have a conversation with you and not offend you. Please forgive me. My intentions are always honorable. I am just afraid my diplomatic skills seem to vanish when I am speaking with you."

Instinctively Amara responded to Keino so powerfully she could only say, "Apology accepted, Keino. I know I am probably being just a little hard on you but you catch me off guard with your extraordinary points of view."

Keino leaned forward in his chair and lowered his voice. The lowered tones sent Amara's senses reeling as he said, "Where I come from, my points of view are not at all extraordinary."

Struggling to maintain an even, composed response Amara replied, "Touché."

The tenuous thread which connected them tightened as Keino spoke. "Amara, I called not to spar with you, but to entice you into spending an evening with me so that I can enjoy your company. By the way, I would like us to spend the evening here in Virginia. You did suggest that, didn't you?"

With a smile in her voice Amara answered, "Yes, I believe I did. An evening spent with you, Keino, would have to be at the very least, interesting."

With a hint of a challenge in his voice Keino asked, "And at the very most, what would it be?"

Not willing to accept the challenge at that moment Amara skillfully answered, "That remains to be seen."

Seizing an opportunity to move forward Keino jumped in, "All right, how about this Friday?"

"Oh—I'm sorry, Keino, but Friday evening my sister Afiya is having an opening at her gallery. I promised I'd be there. Maybe another time?"

Adept as he was at turning seemingly failed situations to his advantage, Keino rushed to save the battle he felt he'd just won. "Oh, no, not so fast. I think I would make a suitable escort to accompany you to the opening—unless someone else has that honor."

Amara could only smile. "No one else is escorting me."

"Wonderful! Then let me have the privilege. At what time shall I call for you?"

"The reception is at seven, the formal showing begins at eight."

"All right then, I'll be around to call for you at six-thirty, Friday evening." Keino paused and then said, "Amara, I am really looking forward to Friday."

"So am I, Keino, so am I."

"Until Friday, then, Amara; enjoy your book!"

"Thank you, Keino. Good night."

"Good night, Amara."

With the end of the conversation came the release of breaths neither of them knew they had held. Amara closed her eyes, hugged her knees to her chest and smiled a long lazy smile. Keino lifted himself from the chair behind his desk where had sat for far too many hours, and with a bit more of a bounce in his step than usual, he headed for home.

Chapter 14

Friday could not come quickly enough for Keino. Bradford flew in for an early business lunch with a group of prospective clients and to play a nine hole round of golf. When they had a moment alone, Keino said to Brad, "Thanks, old man, for the advice. I'm escorting Amara to a gallery opening tonight."

Brad responded in his most congenial manner. "I knew you could pull it off; now, don't blow it."

After the game Keino had just enough time to bid farewell to Brad, go home, shower, dress, and prepare to pick up Amara.

His mood was buoyant. Just the thought of spending time with Amara left him hopefully expectant. He had taken the time during the day to send to her office a profusion of orchids, lilies, glads, and tulips. He attached a note which read: "Their beauty cannot compare to yours. Until tonight. Keino."

The delivery of the enormous bouquet had been the talk of the afternoon among Amara's staff. Amara merely shook her head and smiled, seeing even more clearly evidence of the fact that every gesture that Keino made was indeed larger than life. The more she learned of him the more she wanted to know, but a small voice repeatedly instructed her to be careful.

When Amara arrived home she had just enough time to prepare for Keino to pick her up. Mixed feelings were running amok through her as she pushed the sweeping inner turmoil aside in order to control her exterior and present a picture of deceptive calm for Keino.

When the doorbell rang, she composed herself and went to answer it. Before opening the door, in order to buy herself more time, she looked into the peephole and was treated with a very distorted picture of the man she was longing to see. She opened the door and once again had her breath taken away. His smoldering eyes met her hopeful ones. They both stood mute, feeling a sensuous heat radiating between them. Amara felt a tingling in the pit of her stomach as Keino slowly and seductively visually appraised her, showing great appreciation for her form. Though his gaze was as soft as a caress, his pulse was pounding. Amara broke the silence.

"Welcome to my home, Keino, please come in."

Amara stepped away from the door and from Keino's hard tense body. Keino moved farther into the room, closed the door behind him and said, "Thank you, Amara. Your home is as lovely as its owner."

Amara inclined her head in a gesture of thanks and responded. "Speaking of lovely, thank you so very much for the flowers. The bouquet was magnificent and all of the blossoms you selected are my favorites. How did you know?"

Keino moved closer to Amara and while staring at her intensely he responded, "I make it my business to know everything that pleases you. I want to always please you."

With all the grace of a dancer Amara swirled, stepped back, and asked, "Would you like a glass of wine before we leave?"

As Amara headed to the kitchen, Keino followed her, admiring the gentle sway of her hips. "I'd like that very much—we do have time. Shall I help you pour?"

Amara continued the comfortable banter. "Why, that's very considerate of you. I have a nice light, white wine in the refrigerator; if you'll get it I'll get the glasses."

They worked together in companionable silence as they completed their respective tasks. Keino interrupted the silence. "Amara, before we leave tonight I would like to say something to you."

Amara froze in the moment, looked into Keino's eyes and said, "Yes, Keino, what is it?"

Keino began slowly, his deep vibratos pulsating in Amara's ears. "I am certain you remember the introduction at the banquet of Ms. Makena Rono. I believe my father's words were that one day he hoped she would be a member of our family. Well, I need you to know that Makena Rono will never be my wife. Though there are some traditional debts I must pay, I am free to explore a relationship with any woman I choose, and I choose you; you, Amara Terrell. What I need is your permission to allow me to show you the depths of my feelings for you. One day soon I hope to explain in detail the circumstances of my life, but for now please know that I am free to do as I wish."

"Keino, it all sounds so complex, so involved. I try very hard to eliminate drama from my life, not create it or invite it into my personal life. Drama at work I can handle. Personally, I need peace, harmony. Being involved with you sounds like high drama. I love theater, but not in a relationship."

"You, Ms. Amara Terrell, are making many assumptions. Number one, involvement with me would bring you peace and harmony. Number two, you would be protected from any bit of drama that might explode around me from time to time. Number three, if you feel what I feel, your body, mind, and spirit—not to mention your curiosity—will not allow you to miss the opportunity to explore what we could be. Amara, do us both a favor and put me out of my misery. I have never been treated this badly by a woman. All I am asking is for the opportunity to please you. You are turning me into a beggar, a role with which I am not at all familiar."

In jest Amara responded, "If this is your idea of begging, you have no worries; you have not mastered the part."

Though Keino was amused by Amara's quick retort, he pushed ahead. The moment Amara finished her sentence, he moved so close to her that she could feel his breath whisper like cool wind over the skin on her heated face. He tilted his head to one side and spoke in husky, sensuous tones. "Amara, I am asking again, give me the opportunity to know you and to allow you to know me. I promise you will not regret your decision."

At that moment, Keino took Amara in his arms and began a slow, mind-drugging kiss.

His touch was impossible for her to resist. The kiss which had begun slowly, intensified, embodying the maddening anticipation they had both been holding on to for weeks without gratification. They both drank in the nectar of the kiss. Trembling from the heat of it and the commanding power of Keino's caress, Amara, as if through no will of her own, placed her arms around Keino's strong muscular neck as his fingers, with gentle authority, sensuously played her long arms and the curvature of her back. As their bodies began racing out of control, Keino took the reins and gently moved Amara away from him, attempting to slow the fires raging within them. He raised a single finger, placing a featherlike touch on Amara's chin. "My sweet, either we leave now or we will have to phone in our apologies to your sister for missing the opening."

Reality sank in as Amara, with wide eyes and body still throbbing, stated in a low shivering voice, "If you will just wait here, Keino, I'll go get my wrap and we can be on our way. The last thing I need is to explain my absence tonight."

By the time Keino and Amara arrived at the gallery they were both still draped in a cloak of highly charged sexual magnetism. A dizzying current raced through them. They longed to touch one another. With one kiss, hearts and souls had been unlocked. They found as many ways as they could to be close without being obvious, a surreptitious touch here and there, a whisper in the ear, feigned conversation. All of it barely satisfied the need for the closeness they craved. As they continued walking through the large gathering, Amara finally spotted her sister Afiya. Afiya was a vision wrapped from head to toe in burnished gold cloth with an amber neckpiece and matching earrings.

She was in her element holding forth, describing one of the installations on display. Amara and Keino walked into the group and stood until she finished. When she saw them she rushed over with all of her usual exuberance and greeted Amara and Keino. "Why, hello you two, I am so glad you could make it!"

Afiya and Amara embraced lovingly while Amara spoke. "Afiya, you remember Keino Mazrui?"

"Why, of course I do! Wonderful to have you here, Keino. I hope you enjoy the art. Garvis Lane is making quite a name for himself. His pieces are quite powerful."

As Keino began to speak, Amara could not help but be mesmerized by his virility and his commanding presence. With every syllable she knew that she was slipping into the abyss she knew as Keino. "You are so right, Afiya. As I look at this work I can feel the power of his gift. His piece called *Slavery* is so poignant, one can feel the effects of the middle passage just by looking at the faces of the people. The horror in their eyes speaks volumes."

Afiya spoke eagerly. "That's it, Keino, you saw it! One of the great pleasures of my work is when people get the message of a piece along with its beauty."

Before she could catch herself, Amara said in a broken whisper, "Keino never misses important messages and he seems very adept at giving pleasure."

Both Keino and Afiya looked at Amara simultaneously as if on cue. Afiya's look said, *What pleasure are you talking about Amara?* Keino's look was laced with a smile as he said, "Afiya, please excuse us. I think I'll get Amara a glass of wine."

Amara continued smiling, feeling almost as giddy

as a schoolgirl. Afiya waved them on saying, "Not a problem, you two enjoy the rest of the exhibition."

Before Amara and Keino walked away, Afiya took Amara's hand in hers, touched it gently and said, "Amara, I'll talk to you tomorrow, OK?"

"Yes, Afiya. Don't worry, I am fine. Perhaps better than I've ever been."

Amara and Keino walked away, leaving Afiya smiling and shaking her head.

Keino placed his hand at the small of Amara's slender waist and as they walked he whispered in her ear. "My sweet, as much as I am flattered by your appreciation of my ability to bring you pleasure, I am not sure you should make a public pronouncement."

Amara stared up into Keino's seductive gaze and responded, smiling with a sensuality he could feel in his core. "I know that was so silly of me and so unlike me. It just came out. I don't know what I was thinking. Actually, I wasn't thinking. Keino, the effect you are having on me can't be good. Look at me—one kiss and I'm losing my mind."

A captivating smile played at the corners of his mouth as he replied, "Oh, my sweet, it is my prayer that my kisses will become so commonplace for you the pleasure of them will become an expectation, not a novelty. Since we have made our appearance I think I should take you home—you have much to think about."

Keino led Amara to the exit. As they walked to the door only aware of each other, Robert King, leaning against a pillar, was unseen as he watched them leave. He stood enraged as he saw the woman he had come to see, leaving with another man. Not just any man but the arrogant egomaniac they had run into a few weeks ago at the Ailey concert. Robert King was furious.

By the time Keino and Amara reached the car they were more than happy to be alone, away from the crowd, free to just be a couple to explore the possibilities of being together. As Keino drove and the soft sounds of David Sandborn filtered through the speakers, he turned his head slightly in Amara's direction, placed one hand on her knee and in smooth tones which gently caressed her ears said, "Are you all right, my darling? You appear to be lost in thought."

"I am fine. I must admit, I'm feeling a bit bewildered."

"Bewildered about what, my sweet?"

Amara blurted out, unaware of the sensuousness in her voice, "I suppose I am just surprised at my response to you. Everything about you is new. Every encounter I have with you is unlike any experience I've ever had. I guess I'm just trying to sort it all out."

A briskness permeated his tone as he said, "My precious, fanciful Amara, you may sort for a lifetime and all you will ever see is that you were created for me."

Amara found that thought very satisfying. Her only response was a long soulful look at Keino's sculpted profile and a warm, slow smile. When Keino pulled his car into Amara's driveway for the second time that evening, he silenced his motor and swiveled in his seat to face Amara. With streetlights and the spotlights illuminating Amara's pathway as the only sources of shadowy light, Amara and Keino were left to bask in the glow of one another's eyes. The moment their eyes met, the dance began. They each in turn fell into the smoldering depths of the pools which lay before them. Momentarily unnerved by the prolonged anticipation, Amara blinked, closed her eyes and cast her head down. With light feathery strokes, Keino began to trace a trail from her temple to the edge of her jaw. Amara began to feel a rush of heat tiptoe through her veins. At that moment his hands placed on her shoulders elicited a wave of passion unable to be contained. As she parted her lips to speak his name, Keino's lips found hers and she was shattered by the hunger of his kisses. Her name became a mantra as he devoured the softness of her lips. Their hands began to sear each other as they traced paths down arms and backs, caressing faces as they captured, recaptured, claimed and reclaimed parted lips and explored soft warm flesh.

Keino once again reined in his desires. With a voice heavy with need and wanting Keino began, "My sweet, sweet Amara, once again I must say, if I am to be a gentleman this evening, I must see you to your door now. You, my darling, test all that I am made of. If I don't see you safely inside this instant I am afraid I won't leave. At least not tonight."

His eyebrow rose a fraction and a smile curled the corner of his lips. Amara's body was still aching with longing as she spoke in a low, unconsciously seductive manner. "You are right, Keino, walk with me to my door."

As they stood at the door, holding one another, Amara spoke in what was almost a whisper. "Keino, thank you for going to the opening with me tonight."

"Amara, my sweet, I am always available anytime to take you anywhere you want to go. It is my desire to spend every moment that you will allow with you."

Taking a deep unsteady breath, Keino stepped

back with his hands still placed on Amara's arms, kneading them gently while he spoke. "Amara, you spoke earlier of your experience thus far with me as being unique, new to you. Well, my desire for you, my darling, is beyond anything I have imagined or experienced. Feelings for you wash over me like a volcanic eruption and the molten lava seeps into my soul. I am branded by the sight, scent, and feel of you. You touch my heart, you stir emotions I did not know I had. You make me burn, and I want you in my life." Keino paused, his jaw clenched and his eyes narrowed as he said, "Are you going to give me the opportunity to spend the time it takes for us to explore what we can be together?"

The smile in Amara's eyes reached her lips as she responded, "Yes, Keino, what else can I say but yes."

"Nothing else needs to be said, yes will suffice. I accept your yes, and I think sealing this contract is in order." He kissed her forehead, each eye, the tip of her nose, each check, each earlobe, her chin, and began ravishing her mouth while repeating over and over, "You are mine, Amara, you are mine."

The kiss ended out of necessity. Only the longing as Keino and Amara said good night remained.

Chapter 15

As Amara sat at her breakfast table with the morning sunlight filtering through her bright yellow kitchen, she snuggled in her warm chenille robe and soft quilted slippers while drinking hot tea and catching up on the national news by thumbing through the *Wall Street Journal*. Just as she was about to lift her cup for another sip of her favorite herbal tea, her telephone rang. She got up, picked up her cordless telephone, sat back down, pushed talk and answered in her normal cheery style. Veronica was on the other end of the line. "Good morning Miss Thang and how was the opening. I had a late client so I missed it."

Amara could not stop herself from rushing into a litany of the previous night. "Veronica, I had a great time. Keino is more man than I think I've ever known. There is just so much about him that I like and appreciate. He's warm, bright, funny, compassionate—"

Before Amara could finish Veronica interrupted. "Bottom line, girl, tell me about the chemistry. Is there any? Can the man kiss? I mean, can he *kiss*?"

Amara continued playfully, "Roni, you are never going to change. Here I am trying to tell you about the man's character and you're asking about pleasures of the flesh. You are so nosy; must I tell you everything?"

"Yes."

"OK, if I must, yes he can kiss, only I wouldn't describe what he does as kissing. I've been kissed. Keino beamed me up to another planet. Veronica, I thought I was on *Star Trek*. Remember that episode when Spock was in heat for the woman he was betrothed to and he couldn't function, he couldn't think, he had to go kill somebody and take this woman before he could get back to normal? Well, I didn't feel like killing anybody but my thinking was truly impaired. Thank God Keino is a gentleman, because with very little persuasion I think I would have been his for the taking."

"Oh, my God! Is this Amara Terrell, Miss I'm Going to Wait for My Wedding Night? Girl, I have to meet this Keino. This brother must be good."

"Veronica, he's better than good! Bye, girl, I've got to get to the center. Saturday is here again and my boys are waiting. We'll talk later."

"We sure will. You'd better slow your fast self down or I'm gonna tell your mother."

They both erupted in gales of laugher as they hung up. As soon as Amara put the telephone in its cradle and started to leave her kitchen to get ready for her day, her telephone rang again.

"Hello."

"Hey, sis, how's it going?" Afiya started slowly and spoke with a mysterious edge. "It would appear that I am not the only one who had a grand success last night. Anything you need or want to tell your dear sister?"

"Afiya, you sound like Veronica. I'll tell you what I told her. Keino is a wonderful man whose kisses are better than chocolate. I am going to take the time to get to know and enjoy him."

Breathing a sigh of relief Afiya continued, "Well, sweetheart, you were the one with the reservations. I am all for following your heart. I liked Keino. He has great energy and the two of you are smashing together. I'd say go for it, sis, enjoy this ride wherever it takes you. This looks like a cosmic trip to me. They don't happen very often." Afiya paused pensively before saying, "Love you, sis, I'll probably see you at the center."

Amara, feeling the warmth of her sister's support responded. "Thanks, Afiya. I love you, too."

Amara bounced into the mentoring center. She felt light and gay, still riding on the wave of the excitement she felt being with Keino. She had to smile as she relived her conversations with Veronica and Afiya. She was sure that Afiya couldn't wait to get on the phone to enlighten her other sisters about last night's events. Having sisters could be a joy and a curse—especially if they were your friends in addition to being your sisters. As Amara rounded the corner, headed for the recreation room just to peek to see how the day was shaping up, she was startled by Robert King's long languid figure standing at the entrance of the rec room. His eyes impaled her, they bore into her with an intensity that frightened and unnerved her. Catching her breath and bringing her hand to her chest she asked with irritation and frustration in her voice, "Robert, what on earth are you doing here?"

His tone was chilly as he answered, "Must I have

permission to be here? I thought this was a mentoring center; I thought there were children here who need guidance."

Even more annoyed now, Amara responded, "Robert, you know what I mean. You startled me. What brings you here today? After all, I don't remember you volunteering before."

As Amara attempted to walk past Robert into the recreation room he grabbed her arm so tightly that she winced when he pulled her around while saying, "Amara, I need to speak to you right now!"

Amara stiffened as though he had struck her. She looked into his eyes and knew clearly that she was dealing with a different Robert from the one she thought she knew. Fear grabbed her and held on. In an effort to gain control of the situation, she attempted to calm herself by speaking very calmly and evenly. "Robert, if you want to talk, that's fine. We can always talk. Let's go in the office in the rec room, even though youngsters are working in the room, the office is quiet." She paused, looked at Robert and asked, "Okay?"

Robert agreed. They walked into the rec room. Passing through on the way to the office, Amara was thankful for the time to speak to center participants and continue to calm herself as she headed for the office. Once inside Amara sat, Robert paced. As he began to speak Amara was startled by the things he revealed. "Amara, I saw you at the gallery last night. You were with him. Why did you lie to me Amara? Why did you lie to me?"

"Lie to you? Robert, I have never lied to you, what are you talking about?"

Robert struck his fist on the desk hard causing Amara to jump. "You did lie. You said he was just a new client. Well, since when do clients hold and caress the people they work with the way he did you?"

Amara, continuing in as calm a voice as possible asked, "Robert, why is my personal life of interest to you? I am very confused right now, Robert. Why were you watching me at the gallery? Why didn't you come up and speak to us? When did I lie to you? Robert, you are confusing me and you are scaring me! What is happening?"

"Amara, I feel like a fool. All this time I've waited and hoped and prayed that you would see me and see how much I care for you—how much I love you. It was more than I could take to see you taken in by Mr. Keino Mazuri. When I saw you I knew I could never compete."

Robert slumped in the chair opposite Amara and hung his head in his hands. The only thing Amara could say was, "Robert, I am so sorry, I would never knowingly mislead you. I thought we were lifelong friends. I always valued our friendship, I never misled you. As for Keino, until last night I was not as clear as I needed to be about my feelings for him, and we still have a great deal to sort out and we are just taking a step at a time, a day at a time. Please understand, I would never mislead you. Never."

Robert pulled himself up from the chair, looked at Amara with a blank distant stare and said, "Amara, if I never see you again, have a nice life." With that, he walked out of the office and out of the building.

Amara could still feel her body trembling as she stood to close the office door then sat to calm her nerves. She volunteered the rest of the day in a trance-like state, feeling so sad for Robert and wanting to kick herself for not picking up on the clues he must have left along the way. She should have seen this coming.

When Cassandra and Adana arrived at the center together, Amara was so happy to see them she was almost teary-eyed. As they walked into the rec room where Amara was finishing up a project with one of the mentees Amara looked up and with deep affection and relief said, "Hi, you two. I am really glad to see you today. Before you get started can we walk down to the cafeteria for lattes and conversation?"

"Sounds good to me," Cassandra announced. Adana agreed.

After the sisters had purchased their drinks and seated themselves Adana began the conversation. "Hey, I missed both of you at Afiya's opening last night. There were so many people coming and going. I think it was really successful. I really enjoyed the work."

Cassandra chimed in, "When I got there Afiya said I had just missed both of you. And you, Miss Amara, I am told were so disoriented the magnificent Mr. Mazrui had to take you home to save you from yourself."

That comment made them all laugh. Soon they were giggling like schoolgirls. The gaiety gave Amara the relief she needed. "Yeah, I guess I really had it bad. Keino is just so different. He is quite a man. I could really get used to him."

"Sounds like you already have."

"It's hard to know people, they can be so peculiar, they can fool you. I had the strangest thing happen to me today."

Adana weighed in, firing questions rapidly, "What strange thing? What happened—"

Amara, attempting to slow Adana's naturally quick tongue replied, "Wait just a minute and I'll tell you. Robert came by here today, frantic. He really scared me. He was angry because he saw me with Keino last night. He accused me of leading him on, misleading him about our relationship. I was shocked, frightened, mad. I felt like running, crying, I wanted to slap him. He ranted and raved and finally left in a huff, and told me to have a nice life. He had the strangest look in his eyes, I'll never forget it."

Cassandra and Adana exploded in unison with questions. "What was his problem?"

Adana offered, "Do I need to get a restraining order for your protection?"

Cassandra rushed in. "Is Robert losing his mind?"

"No, I think everything's is okay," was Amara's thoughtful response.

Adana's voice was as cool and as clear as ice water when she said, "See, that's why there is truth to the old saying that men and women can't just be friends. Somebody always wants more."

Amara answered, "Before today I would have disagreed with you. Robert gave me a lot to think about."

Cassandra inquired, "Are you all right now?"

Amara expelled a long audible breath and spoke. "Yeah, I'll be fine. I think I am going home to go to bed. I'll see you two at Mom and Dad's tomorrow." With the end of the conversation Amara left the table and made her way out of the center and headed home.

When Amara left the table, the ever vigilant Adana turned to Cassandra and said, "I don't care what she says, I'm filing a restraining order against Mr. Robert King."

Cassandra added, "I agree, Adana. Better safe than sorry. Robert is sounding a little strange."

Chapter 16

Amara was awakening from a much needed rest from the day's events when the quiet of her home was invaded by the ringing of her telephone. She picked up the phone and answered with a lazy, "Hello."

Keino responded with, "Hello, my sweet. How are you today?"

Hearing his voice brought a calm and a peace over Amara which she didn't realize she was missing. "I'm fine, Keino. How are you?"

"Well, lovely one, I am finishing up a bit of weekend business and I decided I would entice you into an early dinner. Is that a possibility?"

"OK, I think that is a distinct possibility. I can't think of anything I'd enjoy more at this moment."

"You can't? In that case, should I attempt to expand your imagination?"

"Keino Mazrui, can we just enjoy the dinner?"

"As you wish, my sweet. Be prepared for a very relaxing casual dinner. I'll send a car for you at five P.M. Until then, my angel."

Keino hung up, leaving Amara anticipating what he had in store for the evening.

At exactly five P.M. Amara's doorbell rang and when she answered she found on her doorstep a uniformed chauffeur explaining that his waiting car was to take her to Keino. As the comfortable late model Lincoln Town Car rode smoothly down the highway, Amara excitedly wondered where she was being taken. Just as she was about to ask the driver for a clue as to her destination, he began driving in the direction of the Potomac River. After about a mile he stopped the car in front of a magnificent yacht docked in its berth. Amara knew she was in for quite an evening.

As she stepped from the door the chauffeur had opened for her, she saw Keino waving to her from the boarded walkway alongside the yacht. They were a matched pair dressed for the cool evening breezes, both in wool trousers and cashmere sweaters. Amara's ensemble was the color of ivory linen while Keino's pants and sweater were a pearl gray. As Amara continued walking towards Keino he stopped waving and immediately fell into a very commanding stance with legs apart and both arms outstretched with palms turned upward, waiting to be filled with Amara's downturned hands. Once they clasped hands Amara's automatic response was to glide into Keino's arms, fitting his torso like a missing puzzle piece. They kissed as only they could, savoring the newness, never wanting it to end. Keino was the first to speak. "Welcome aboard, my darling, welcome to another one of my pleasures. I hope you enjoy dinner on the water. I felt like being removed from land tonight. Being near water soothes and relaxes me."

"I love the water," was Amara's relaxed response.

"Keino, you are really full of surprises. How long have you had this beautiful vessel?"

"I bought it when I first came to Virginia. I had expected to spend a great deal more time enjoying it, but that has not happened yet. I learned to really appreciate the power and the beauty of being in and around the water in college. During my studies in London, I was a part of the rowing team, and I have done my share of waterskiing and playing water polo. As I said, there is something about water. It calms the spirit."

Amara's eyes sparkled and she asked, "Keino, is there anything you can't do?"

Keino's mischievous retort made Amara smile. "Well, if I remember correctly, I couldn't convince you to meet me in Curacao. Does that count?" Keino gave her a sidelong glance with a crooked smile, grabbed her hands and gently commanded, "Come, my pet, let's go below for dinner."

Keino's yacht, like its owner, epitomized understated elegance. A powerfully built vessel, it was sleek and luxurious. A tri-deck yacht, it was equipped with Keino's private suite on the main deck and a second deck which provided a VIP suite, three guest cabins and a gym. The third deck housed a spacious living room and an elegant formal dining room. A sky lounge was housed on deck two, along with a fly bridge which provided scenic entertainment areas for relaxation and enjoyment. This was indeed an exquisite sailing machine. As Amara was led to Keino's shipboard dinning room she expressed her pleasure. "Keino, this is all so very beautiful. As we came down the stairs I couldn't help but notice the wonderful display of photos of jazz artists in your hallway art gallery. Another surprise—I didn't realize you were such a jazz lover.

My father made my sisters and me cut our teeth on jazz. My mother often says he didn't play lullabies for us, he played Miles, Coltrane, Charlie Parker, and countless others, some so obscure it seemed only my father knew them."

"Your father was correct to do that. Since it is one of the major art forms created by an African people, we must preserve its legacy. Do you not agree?"

Amara inclined her head toward Keino, looked deeply into his eyes and said, "I do indeed agree. I can also see that you are a man of many passions."

Keino focused his gaze on Amara, lowered his silken voice and responded, "That may be, but tonight I am interested in the pursuit of only one of my passions."

As Keino spoke his eyes never left hers as he directed Amara to a chair at the stunningly appointed dining room table. Once she was seated, a gentleman's butler appeared and began to serve them a delectable meal of marinated shrimp with snow peas, curried chicken, cucumber hearts with sun-dried tomatoes, and wild rice with shitake mushrooms. Fresh strawberries and cream served as dessert and champagne from Keino's private reserve accompanied the meal.

"Keino, you really have outdone yourself. Everything was scrumptious."

While holding a fluted glass in his hand, his eyes caressed her softness. "I am happy to have pleased you. Your wish is my command."

Those words made Amara think of the encounter with Robert King. She dropped her eyes and began speaking. "The last person who said that to me is not only no longer my friend, but he thinks I betrayed him and wants me to burn in hell."

Keino's eyes widened in alarm, his back became ramrod straight, his voice piercing. "What's this? What are you saying?"

Amara continued, needing the cathartic release of letting go of one she had treasured as a dear friend. "A person I thought was a dear friend turned on me today. Robert King, you met him. He and I went to the Alvin Ailey concert together, you were there. We ran into you, remember?"

Keino calmed himself before answering, but his tone was laced with icy contempt. "Oh, I remember very well. I was disappointed seeing you with another man after you had so soundly rejected my offer to Curacao. But I must admit, at least I was happy to be face-to-face with my competition."

Exasperated that Keino seemed more concerned about Robert as his competition than as her lost friend, Amara expressed her irritation. "Men! Just stop, Keino; Robert was my friend, not my lover, nor was he your competition. I thought he was clear about our friendship. Boy, was I wrong. At first I was angry, and frightened, then hurt. I couldn't believe my intentions could have been so misunderstood."

With a seductively maddening hint of arrogance, Keino replied, "My sweet, friendship between men and women is a very tricky business. In the West, too many lines are blurred. It makes for much confusion."

"Keino, I don't care about blurred lines. I thought Robert and I were clear. We've known each other for years."

"My sweet, you are an extremely desirable woman,

and in my humble opinion there are few men alive who would not want you. Some may not be as honest about it as I have chosen to be. Now tell me, Amara, where did this encounter take place?"

"Today at the mentoring center."

With a lethal calm in his eyes and a deadly seriousness in his tone Keino asked, "Shall I impress upon Mr. King that he is never to cause you anguish again?"

As his burning eyes held her still, Amara rushed to reassure him. "Oh, Keino, no, no. It will be fine."

Keino lightened his air, placed his arm around Amara, and said, "If you say so, my sweet. Now come with me to the observation deck, the night is clear, and I desire to see your face reflected in the moonlight."

He made a mental note to have a message delivered to Mr. Robert King.

Amara and Keino walked arm and arm up the spiral staircase to the observation deck of the yacht. Once there, Keino began to speak while holding Amara in his arms. "My darling Amara, I cannot begin to tell you how good it feels to be with you tonight. Thank you for accepting my invitation. I want to spend many days and nights in your presence. We need time alone together. My original trip to Curacao was postponed because of a business snafu. Those details have been worked out and I need to once again make the trip. I need you with me. I have to leave before you, but I will make arrangements for you as I offered before. You will be my guest with every possible convenience at your disposal. You have two days to make your decision. I leave tomorrow."

Keino was so compelling that Amara's body felt

heavy and warm; she looked into his eyes and her heart raced. She could feel his heart beating against her own. The sensuality of the moment flooded in on both of them, as they gently swayed in the slight breeze of the evening. As Keino whispered his plea into her hair, Amara felt her spirit leave her body. Keino's mouth covered hers hungrily.

Chapter 17

After leaving Keino's yacht, Amara spent a very restless night agonizing over making a decision about whether or not to accompany Keino to Curacao. She knew this was a choice that would change the course of her life, however it worked out. Keino had promised her nothing. He had offered her much materially, but he had not talked about giving of himself except in the most carnal sense. Yes, she was clear that he wanted her, but for how long? Was she willing to share with Keino the two things she had never shared with another man, her body and her soul? A part of her wanted so much to take the opportunity to be with Keino. She had nothing to lose by going. Her heart told her to call her administrative assistant and put her affairs in order, and get on that plane. Her logical mind told her not to be foolish, not to be impulsive, not to give in to crazy whims. As the dawn broke her decision was made. As the early morning light shone through her window Amara knew she had to go.

* * *

When the day arrived for Amara to fly to Curacao, she bathed, dressed, packed, and called Melissa Etheridge, her Administrative Assistant. Melissa was a naturally optimistic, perky person. She was medium height, more ample figured than she wished to be, extremely efficient and unquestionably loyal to Amara. When Melissa heard Amara's voice her pecan toned face lit up, ready to begin the work of the day.

It was Melissa's habit to get into the office before the early morning traffic. She was single and quite free to move about as she chose. Much of her life revolved around her work and so she responded with her usual good humor to Amara's requests to handle specific tasks while she was away.

After handling the last minute office duties Amara phoned her parents. She had purposely waited until the final hour to let them and her sisters know that she was leaving. She wasn't ready to face questions or hear herself try to explain her actions until they made sense to her.

She chatted with her mother, as was her custom at least three times per week. During this conversation, she told her mother that she was taking a very spur of the moment trip to Curacao. She did not dare say what for. The unspoken assumption was that the trip was for business. Though all of her children were grown women, Ana Terrell expected a certain level of decorum never to be breached. She had no desire to be privy to the ways in which her daughters handled their love lives. After their good-byes were said, Ana turned to her husband as he dressed for the lecture he was to give at the university. Ana spoke. "James, Amara sent her love."

"Oh, good, how is she?"

"Fine. She's on her way to Curacao. Though it was not stated, we are to assume it's business."

"What do you mean 'we are to assume'?"

"Oh, James, I don't know, I just feel as though there is more to this trip than we're being told."

"She's a big girl, baby, she can handle herself. She's a smart cookie. You know we didn't raise any dimwits."

"Yes, my love, I know. I gave them the perfect father, they can only do well."

They embraced as they had for years with all the fervor that held them together through all of their marital experiences.

As Amara rode to the airport in the car Keino had sent for her, she tried futilely to stop her heart from racing. Mixed emotions of fear and excitement were simultaneously warring within her. She was having a difficult time containing her joy at the thought of seeing Keino again. She was also very anxious to hear him clear up what he called misconceptions, and most of all, she was afraid of what could happen when they were alone miles away from prying eyes.

As the car pulled into the section of the airport reserved for private aircraft, it slowed to a stop next to a seven-thirty-seven jet airliner with a majestic "M" emblazoned on its tail and Mazrui Industries written on its side. Had she not already experienced Keino Mazrui in the flesh, she might have been utterly overwhelmed, but knowing Keino, how could anyone expect less? As she was smiling broadly wondering how many other surprises Keino had in store for her, she was approached by the pilot, in

full dress uniform, who, as he came closer, seemed
vaguely familiar to her. She had a quizzical look on
her face as Kaleb approached her. With hand extended for the traditional Western greeting he
smiled and said, "Hello, Ms. Terrell, welcome a-
board. I am Kaleb Mazrui, Keino's younger brother
and your pilot. We have been given strict instruc-
tions to make sure that this is the most comfortable
flight you have ever taken."

"Thank you so much," Amara responded, beaming. "I must say, I can see the family resemblance."

Kaleb nodded, smiled, and stepped aside as
Amara boarded the plane. As she walked through
the door he laughed to himself, thinking, *Makena,
you don't have a chance. When my brother said take care
of this woman, he meant take care of his woman.*

Whether Amara knew it or not, in Kaleb's eyes
she had Keino Mazrui stamped all over her. At that
moment, Amara entered the cabin of the plane
and was transfixed. It was as well appointed as a
luxury hotel suite. A well equipped galley, a living
room furnished with plush bronze leather sofas
and matching chairs. There were also rosewood
cocktail tables, state-of-the-art TV, VCR, DVD and
sound system, and beyond her view a most beautifully decorated bedroom and two bathrooms with
gold framed mirrors, rosewood vanities, and glass
enclosed marble showers.

As she took her seat the attendant entered from
the galley, introduced herself, and informed Amara
that immediately after takeoff she would be given
a menu from which to select her luncheon meal.
Amara thanked the attendant and settled back for
the flight and thoughts of Keino.

As Amara leaned back and prepared to soothe
her nerves, Kaleb, in the cockpit, heard the ring of

his personal telephone. He looked at the face of it and smiled seeing what he recognized as Keino's private line. Kaleb's answer to the ring was, "Hey, big brother, I think I have precious cargo on board that might interest you."

"Is that right?" Keino responded. "I am pleased that she decided to come."

Kaleb quipped, "And now I see why you are not running to marry Makena."

Keino jumped in, "Hold on, brother, I just met this woman. My decision not to marry Makena had nothing to do with Amara."

"I hear you, brother, you said had nothing to do with your marrying Makena. She might not have had anything to do with it but I'll bet she has something to do with it now." And with that observation he roared with laughter.

"OK, Kaleb, you stick to flying and I'll handle my personal life. Have the attendant put me through to Amara."

"You've got it, big brother. By the way, I like your choice."

"Kaleb, Kaleb, just put me through," said Keino with laughter still ringing in his voice.

Just as Amara had closed her eyes waiting for takeoff clearance, the attendant softly touched her shoulder and announced, "Ms. Terrell, Mr. Keino Mazrui is on the line for you."

Amara whispered a "thank you," to the attendant and, steeling herself against the rush of heat she felt radiate throughout her body she picked up the receiver, sighed, and said, "Hello, Keino, how are you?"

The sexual magnetism was evident even over the telephone wires as he said, "I am fine now that I know you are on the plane. I have missed seeing your exquisite face, hearing your lovely voice and seeing that smile which puts the sun to shame."

"Keino, what am I going to do with you?"

"As soon as you land, I will show you," he said with a hint of mischief in his voice. He was so devastatingly appealing and his voice was affecting her deeply. She felt herself hanging on to her emotions by a tenuous thread. His erotic promise to show her what to do with him had only helped to fan the flames. Keino continued, "I promised you an itinerary which the attendant has. You know you are free to discard it if you wish. Your time away from me is your own. You are free to do as you wish. But Amara, you must know that when we are together on this trip, your time is mine. When we are together I will determine how we spend our time. The only thing I will not control is your body. When, and if, I am ever allowed the privilege of searing a path down your honey colored throat, or parting your luscious lips, or thrusting into you like a raging fire, it will be because your hunger has equaled mine."

She shivered. Her entire body was raging and pulsating at the visual image Keino painted. She had no idea that she was capable of such passion, but then she had never met Keino Mazrui before. Before she had time to collect herself to respond, she heard Keino say, "Until then my sweet," and he was gone.

Chapter 18

As the plane descended, Amara could not remember when she had seen terrain more beautiful. She was delighted that she had consented to come. The description of her living arrangements, and the itinerary of her stay had been given to her on the plane, but neither had prepared her for the lavish way in which Keino welcomed her to Curacao.

She was driven to a private villa. It was large enough to accommodate a dozen people, though it had been reserved exclusively for her. The grounds were veritable gardens exploding with a wealth of varieties and hues of indigenous plants and flowers. The villa itself was a newly built structure, painted in serene aqua and trimmed in alabaster. A deck, the color of translucent opal, wrapped around the length of the house. The deck was furnished with chaise lounges, chairs and tables made of the finest, tightly woven, ginger colored wicker. The lounges and chairs were plushly upholstered in varying shades of chartreuse and aquamarine. The glass-topped tables were equipped with canvas umbrellas in brightly colored shades of lapis lazuli, periwinkle, and celadon.

The expansive deck provided unencumbered views of sandy beaches and pristine azure waters. The entire effect was, for Amara, as calming as chimes softly swaying and tinkling in a gentle breeze. The sun was shining brightly overhead and there was a slight breeze. As she stepped into the foyer of the villa, the wind whispered through the chalky-white shutters and waved over her bare arms and legs with a feathery caress. At that moment as Keino's face floated through her consciousness the driver spoke. He was an austere man and he appeared more like a bodyguard than a chauffeur. "Ms. Terrell, Mr. Mazrui asked me to let you know that he has left a message for you in the drawing room." Amara thanked the driver, watched him place her bags inside and disappear as quietly as he had entered.

Amara felt very much at ease as she strolled through the foyer and entered the drawing room which lay ahead of her. The interior of the villa was enormously spacious, with architecturally clean uncluttered lines. There were splashes of color on sofas, chairs and rugs, set against stark white walls. As Amara moved through the rooms she saw on a glass-topped Parsons table an envelope with her name inscribed on the outside.

As she read the note, she could feel his touch in every word.

Dearest Amara,

　　If you are reading this hastily penned note, may I say welcome to another of my hideaways. It is paradise. I want you to enjoy it. Everything has been provided for your four-day retreat, a cook, house-

keeper, and a driver. If there is anything else you desire, the housekeeper Mrs. Dollard can be told. I will be residing in another villa on our property approximately one mile from you. William Chin, the driver, will bring you to me at six this evening. Until then, you will be in my thoughts.

As she finished reading the note she marveled at Keino's thoughtfulness. Still holding the note in her hand, surveying the bold commanding penmanship, she heard footsteps, looked up and saw Mrs. Dollard—a round smiling woman the color of sunbaked earth—approaching her, saying in the clipped accent of the island, "Bon bini, welcome, welcome. I am Dinah Dollard. I am going to take care of you."

"Thank you so very much, Mrs. Dollard. The island is so beautiful and so peaceful."

"Yes, it is, you must enjoy yourself. I will take care of everything. You go up to your room and get more comfortable to enjoy the island. The beach is calling your name," she said with a hearty laugh. "Your room is the first door at the top of the stairs. Your bags are already there. Enjoy!" With that, Mrs. Dollard moved away with incredible speed for one with her girth.

Amara climbed the stairs and entered not a bedroom but a suite. The bedroom had within it a blonde four-poster bed draped in gold toned chiffon netting, a sitting area with matching blonde and ashwood chaise, wingback chairs and matching ottoman covered in silk the color of burnished jonquil. The bathroom, tiled in gold toned marble, housed its own whirlpool tub, etched glass, enclosed shower, and sitting and dressing areas.

Every room in the house spoke to who Keino was. A man of means with immense style and a generous heart. She decided to take Mrs. Dollard's advice and change for the beach. She removed her white linen espadrilles and her white linen, spaghetti-strapped knee length sundress. Feeling the cool breeze wash over her as she stood in her strapless white lace bra and matching bikini cut panties she twirled around the room smiling to herself, completely thrilled that she had made the trip and overjoyed at the prospect of seeing Keino again. She hoped she could contain herself until six o'clock.

She showered and put on a French cut, honey colored, backless swimsuit almost the color of her skin; it complimented her curvaceous body, highlighting her perfectly shaped, extraordinarily long legs and her small waist. She headed for the beach, which was a stone's throw from the villa.

The water was blue and clear, unsoiled by the drama of human life. As she stretched out her fluffy white towel on a multicolored beach chair preparing to sit and bask in the sun, a long shadow was cast over the area in which she stood. She looked around and her heart skipped as she focused on Keino standing there. She would never become accustomed to his raw power. There he stood, glistening with the wash of a thin film of perspiration over his ebony face. He was wearing a gauzy milk-colored, collarless shirt unbuttoned from his neck to his navel. The hem of his shirt hung loosely over stark white pants, his feet were shod in ivory linen slip-ons, he was sockless. The passion they both felt seeing one another again was like steam on smoldering asphalt. Keino's eyes burned into Amara as he savored the view of her tantalizing body. He wanted this woman so badly. She elicited in him feelings of virility he had never before experienced. The mixture of lust, want, need, greed and the longing to possess and protect were all thrown together in a turbulent mountain of desire. The swimsuit that she wore allowed him for the first time to see the bare expanse of the legs that set him on fire. He was barely holding onto his treasured self-control. As he silently drew her into his strong wanting arms, he caressed her so gently that she felt as if she were floating, and with such power that she could feel her blood run like hot liquid through her veins. She felt herself dissolving in his hands as he applied light feathery strokes from the base of her neck to her highly sensitized earlobes. He used the center of his thumbs to brush her forearms while whispering, "You are so beautiful, I have wanted to touch you like this since the day I met you. There were things I promised you on the plane that I would not do until you allowed me the privilege. Touching you was not one of them."

He held her closer. Their soft cores were perfectly matched as both of his hands held her to him while he stroked her back with the hands of a master sculptor creating his finest work. His hands, though gentle and warm, sent chills through Amara causing a slight tremor in her limbs which they could both feel, heightening the sensuality, and the pleasure of the moment. Feeling the hardness of his own body and the trembling of Amara's, Keino whispered in her ear, "My beautiful Amara, has your passion equaled mine?"

Amara was so engulfed by the raw electricity she felt, she could not speak. Her breathing was so erratic, all she could do was to raise her palms toward his face and through clouded eyes and halted speech say in an almost inaudible tone, "Keino, please, no."

Keino, ever so gently, moved her from him and whispered again, "I will be ready when you are, my sweet. Time has always been my ally." He touched her mouth lightly with two fingers and said, "Until this evening."

As he walked away, Amara felt all of her doubts drain away. Her soul had surrendered with the first touch. As she continued to watch his elegant strides fade into the distance she knew that she could spend the rest of her life with Keino.

As Keino walked away he was clear now about two things: one, how he should feel when he touched his wife, and two, that he didn't care where Amara was born, he wanted her for a lifetime. His job now was to convince her.

Chapter 19

Keino sent a car to drive Amara to a quaint little supper club called The Breeze. As Amara entered, she noticed that the club was empty. Void of people, but beautifully decorated. There were only ten tables in the room, each designed to seat two. The white linen tablecloths and napkins were gleaming in the candlelit room. Orchids served as the table centerpieces and the golden place settings picked up the bronze tones in the silk upholstered Louis XIV chairs. As she stood in the middle of the room deciding where to sit, it dawned on her that once again Keino showed how important his privacy was to him. He was fond of secluded places. Just as she completed the thought she heard the sounds of violins fill the air and as if on command, Keino entered wearing traditional African dress, a sapphire colored grand bou bou trimmed in silver with matching slippers. Once again, he took her breath away.

"How are you?" He smiled, took her hand, and led her to the center table.

Amara answered, "I am fine, the island is so beautiful I could feel my whole being respond to its beauty the moment I arrived."

"One beauty deserves another," Keino said while sensually kissing her hand. Keino continued, his mood more relaxed than she had ever seen him. "When I saw you earlier today my sense of propriety left me. I apologize. Forgive me. I should have inquired about your health, your well-being, the comfort of the trip, but when I saw you all I knew was that I wanted you. You can see now how you affect me."

Keino was for Amara a mysterious man. Just when she thought she had him figured as a stoic, straight-laced guy he proved to be lighthearted and so willing to be vulnerable. As their eyes met Amara said, "Keino, you are such a special man. I really appreciate your kindness and your generosity. I'll never forget it."

Keino responded while touching Amara's arm with wispy strokes, "And I will gladly hold you to that statement. Let's have dinner. The restaurant is ours tonight. I wanted us to have uninterrupted time because there is a great deal I wish to share with you; there is also so much I wish to know about you," he said with an intensity and force that did not escape her.

"I took the liberty of having a traditional Ethiopian meal prepared in honor of your Ethiopian connection." He tilted his head to one side, and smiled flashing chalk-white teeth against chocolate skin.

"Thank you Keino," Amara said, unable to contain her pleasure. "I love Ethiopian food. One of my favorite restaurants at home is a wonderful Ethiopian restaurant called Horn of Africa."

"I should have known," said a beaming Keino. "You are a woman of many surprises. I know then that you will enjoy the doro wat, injera, and assorted vegetables."

"Doro wat is one of my favorite dishes."

"And you," said Keino, "are one of my favorite people."

Amara lowered her eyes while looking at Keino, smiled broadly and said her thank yous.

Several impeccably dressed waiters served the elegantly prepared meal, leaving Amara and Keino's palates thoroughly satisfied. During the meal, Keino and Amara playfully engaged in the Ethiopian custom of feeding one another morsels of food. Amara explained to Keino that she had heard it said that if lovers feed one another they would be connected forever. Keino laughed and reminded her that they were not yet lovers in the technical sense but that he was willing to oblige if she needed authenticity. Her eyes flew wide open in amazement—she couldn't control her laughter, which was contagious for Keino. In the throes of laugher she found herself in Keino's arms, laughing into the expanse of his strong unyielding chest while he stroked her back. By the time she noticed that he was no longer laughing, he was pulling her to her feet saying, "Come we must talk."

As they walked toward the door, Keino embraced Amara, softly drinking in her scent and feeling the satiny softness of her skin. He was grateful that her black silk, strapless dress left portions of her upper body uncovered, affording him the pleasure of looking and touching. Once they were outside Keino told the driver, who had been waiting, to remain in place while they walked, and he and Amara began a walk along the beach. It was a balmy evening.

The sweet scents of clean water and ambrosial mixtures of various flowers crept through the air. After walking a few hundred yards, Keino led Amara to a bench. He sat down and pulled her onto his lap, assuring her that his lap would be far more comfortable than the wooden slats of the bench. Amara obliged him, though they both knew the decision to do so had nothing to do with the kind of comfort of which he spoke. Keino began, "Amara, until I met you I was willingly, though slowly, following the path that had been set for my personal life. I had resigned myself to the inevitability of a marriage which was on my part, not much more than a business arrangement." Amara listened, transfixed, with her breath caught in her throat.

"I would have married because it is time for me to be about the business of fulfilling my obligation to the extension of my family line. Makena's family and mine have ties which stretch back generations. Though there are no longer legal contractual agreements struck between families as in days of old, verbal commitments are still adhered to; but if the agreements are found not to be to the liking of the parties involved, there are ways out of these agreements which diminish the embarrassment to the families concerned. Though the old legalistic ways have been outlawed, no government can outlaw culture. The old ways will always follow us, however modified to fit contemporary times. I am saying this to let you know that because of meeting you I know what I have to do. Your presence has made it so clear that my home cannot be shared with a woman for whom my soul does not burn. You, Amara, are my fire."

Amara took a long breath. Keino placed his lips

at the base of her throat as she tenderly stroked his head. His touch on her bare back was hypnotic. Keino continued, raising his eyes to meet hers. "I am asking for time to spend with you, to know you, and for you to know me. I need to know if the fire will continue to consume us or if it will burn away and leave us both cold. One might say that I am being presumptuous describing the feelings that exist between us, but I am an astute judge of character. I have spent my life reading people. I know I am not wrong. Your feelings are as clear to me as my own. If I have misread you, please tell me so that I can leave you, because if I am right, I promise never to let you go."

Keino saw Amara's eyes glisten wet with unshed tears. She had been so moved, so touched by his words that she knew she would love him for the rest of her life. She heard Keino say, "Amara, my darling, please don't cry. I need you to talk to me, share with me the desires of your heart."

He set her on her feet and stood facing her. She placed her arms around his neck and parted her lips to speak, but the words fell away as he brushed his lips against hers. They opened together to receive the divine nectar for which they had been waiting. The dance they performed while kissing and stroking left them longing and wanting. Prolonging the expectation of the intimacy they both desired left them soaring, wrapped in a blazing urgency. Taking the reins as was his custom, Keino began to slow the pace. He kissed each eyelid, each earlobe, each corner of Amara's mouth, all the while whispering, "Speak to me, Amara, tell me what you want for us."

Speaking was difficult for Amara. She ached for

his magical touch. She wanted to feel his strong capable hands command every inch of her. She wanted to be his forever. She replied, "Keino, I am afraid. You are right, I want to be with you in a way I have never wanted to be with anyone, but I am so afraid."

His look was a caress as he asked, "Afraid of what?"

With tears streaming down her cheeks she confessed, "Afraid of not fitting into your world, of having our conversations go from sharing laughter and joy to a series of miscommunications based on cultural differences. I don't think I could stand to come to a place where we hated instead of loved."

"Amara, my sweet Amara," he said, holding her close. "I would be lying if I said I didn't have my reservations at first, but I have been watching and listening for weeks now and there is more that connects us than will ever separate us. Trust me, my darling, everyone and everything in both our worlds will welcome our being together."

Tired from the emotionally draining conversation, she asked in a hoarse whisper, "Keino, what about Makena, and what about your parents? I saw Makena and I heard your father."

"Amara, Makena has been told. I have just not formally met with her parents. My father will always assist me in doing what is right for me. He merely wants me to do things in ways that are respectful. My sweet, do not worry your head about this business. It will be handled."

Keino picked up Amara and he cradled her in his arms as she laid her head on his shoulder and he carried her down the beach where he knew his driver would be waiting. When the driver saw them he quickly opened the door and Keino placed Amara on the seat. She slid over and he slid in beside her and they were driven in silence with Amara in Keino's arms to her villa.

Chapter 20

As the car slowed to a stop in front of the villa where Amara was staying, Keino and Amara looked deeply into each other's eyes, knowing clearly where they were headed. Fighting to control her whirling emotions, Amara asked Keino if he would like to come in for a nightcap. Pleasantly surprised and highly aroused by her invitation, Keino consented. As they stepped from the car Keino told his driver that he would walk the distance to his villa later in the evening. The driver accepted that as a command to leave and drove away. As they entered the house, Keino turned on soft lighting and even softer music. When the soft low sounds of a saxophone filled the room he grabbed Amara with the force of a possessive lover and pulled her to him and said, "Tonight I missed the opportunity to dance with you. Now the timing is perfect."

He molded her to him like a well-made glove covering a waiting hand. A sensuousness radiated through them, flooding them both with memories of longing and heated expectations. Their silence held vivid sounds of passion. Amara was over-whelmed by Keino's touch and by the thoughts rushing through her head. She knew that this was the man to whom she would surrender her soul. Her passion, she was sure, had now equaled his. As if reading her mind he lowered his head, lifted her chin, and kissed her with a fire neither of them had ever known. With her arms encircling Keino's neck, he was given free rein to gently stroke the highly sensitive areas of her breasts as he easily slid his thumbs past the top of her strapless dress. Amara whimpered at the touch, feeling a quiver at the center of her being. Keino answered each whimper with small bites to her lips and earlobes while telling her in the most intimate ways how she was making him feel. In tones that hinted of the fire he felt Keino asked, "My darling Amara, has your passion equaled mine?"

Amara heard herself say "yes" repeatedly until the sound was but a whisper, and her body ached for his touch. At that moment he took her hand and led her to the master bedroom.

When they entered the room, Keino, in a vibrato, filled with desire said, "Amara, please turn on a lamp; I must see how beautiful you are."

Amara for the first time felt anxious. She dropped her eyes and took a deep cleansing breath. Keino, feeling the change in her mood, came to her and embraced her from behind, leaving a trail of light feathery kisses all along her honey colored neck, causing her body to tremble and her voice to quiver as she said, "Keino, make love to me now."

Keino looked at her, searching her face and examining her eyes and said, "Amara, we will savor this night. There may be other times when we will be consumed by the heat of passion but tonight, my love, I am going to savor every inch of you."

He quietly released the zipper in the back of her dress while kissing her deeply. When the zipper was undone he stepped back and helped Amara to step from her dress. When he saw her he was speechless. The blazing fire that she saw in his eyes almost frightened her until his gaze softened, he shook his head, smiled and said, "You are the most beautiful woman I have ever seen. You are my perfect Amara."

Amara stood there wearing only black lace bikini panties. Her perfectly round breasts, tiny waist, smooth satin skin and mile long legs were more than he had imagined. As Amara started toward the bed he gently pulled her back to him saying, "No, my sweet, let me savor you a bit longer."

Around and around he circled her form, entranced by its magnificence. Amara was astounded by his attraction to her. His intense approval of her made her love him even more. She melted as his eyes examined every private inch of her.

He picked her up, sat her on the bed, and removed her black lace panties. When they were cast aside Amara wanted to close her eyes but Keino's obvious pleasure in undressing her and reveling in what he saw as her beauty made her feel so feminine, so warm, so wanted and so protected, that she could not help but watch his pleasure. And so, she lay there aching, burning and quivering while he stroked and kissed her center and kissed and suckled each breast. When he stopped she was beside herself with longing, she wanted him. She wanted all of him. She felt as though her body were on fire. As he started to raise himself from the bed to undress, Amara put her arms around his neck and pleaded with him not to leave. He assured her that he was not leaving her, not tonight, not ever. He began to remove his clothes in order to join her in bed. Piece by piece he discarded his garments until there he stood in the soft glow of the lamp. Keino was a vision of virility. He was masculinity personified, strong, hard, perfectly formed arms and legs, washboard abs, taut skin the color of a gloriously starless night, and an aroused manhood as magnificently formed as he was. Taking it all in sent ripples through the core of Amara's being.

When he slid in bed next to her it was like placing kindling on a blazing fire. They were consumed by one another. Their bodies were so intertwined, touching and tasting, there were times when they felt as if they had melted together.

Keino repeated Amara's name as though it were a chant as he suckled, stroked, and caressed her. Amara was engulfed by the electricity of his touch, the erratic rhythm of her heart and the heat that was enveloping her, and then he began to enter her with all of the finesse of a master. As she flinched and became still in his arms he was struck by his inability to move any farther. He stopped, held Amara close while he looked in her now tear-laced eyes. He questioned, "My darling, why did you not tell me that you have never been made love to?"

Tearfully Amara explained, "I didn't want to have you think that something was wrong with me and I didn't want a man of the world to think he had to train a poor, pitiful, sheltered girl."

He said with confusion registering on his face, "How, my darling, did you think you were going to hide this from me?"

"I don't know, I don't know," she said, almost screaming.

Keino wrapped her in his arms and whispered, "It's all right, it's all right. I will take care of you. Don't worry, don't cry," he said. "I am honored that you would bless me with such a gift. Amara, you are a special woman in more ways than I can count. Here, my sweet, just let me hold you. I want your memories of this experience to be joyous. I am so sorry, my darling, I wish you had told me. I could have prepared myself for you instead of taking you like a raging bull."

Keino continued lightly stroking Amara's back and her arms and kissing her eyes with soft, silk-like touches. Thinking out loud he asked, "How have the men in America been able to ignore your beauty? How did you manage, my darling, to be saved for me?" With a grand laugh he questioned, "Do the ancestors love me so much that they would intervene on my behalf to God and He would save you untouched all for me?" The more he talked the more intense he became until he was sitting up in the bed looking down at Amara with a mixture of bliss and admiration. "Please tell me, my darling, how did this blessing befall me?"

Amara sat up in the bed and put her arms around Keino's neck, kissed him softly on the cheek and said, smiling playfully, with a tear-streaked face, "Keino Mazrui, you are the only man in the world who would turn this situation into a plus instead of a minus." Turning her tone to a more serious one she said, "There is no mystery as to how I managed not to have made love. Five years ago I was engaged. It had been my desire to have the perfect wedding and the perfect wedding night, and so I wanted to wait until the actual night of my wedding to make love to my husband for the first time."

Keino continued listening, staring deeply into Amara's eyes. "My fiancé humored me and went along with the program. It wasn't difficult for him to do because none of the passion I've experienced with you was ever a part of our relationship, and for him, his work was more important than anything. He always felt he had something to prove. He wanted to be the nation's top corporate lawyer. When I decided being his wife was not going to be a pleasant life I called off the wedding, and I think in some way he was relieved. I think a wife would have been a distraction for him. Until now, I never considered sharing my body or my soul with anyone else."

As he looked at Amara and listened to her, Keino was consumed with passion by the thought of the one woman in the world who made his heart sing being saved for him to love for the first time. As they both sat up in the bed, Keino placed Amara sideways on his lap and began a kiss which deepened with each touch and passionate whisper. As the kiss deepened over and over again her core shattered into a million pieces, leaving her panting and wanting more. Keino obliged her by taking each in its turn one erect nipple after the other to wash with nips and erotic pulls, leaving her drugged and wanting. As he touched her thigh while nibbling on her mouth and earlobes she felt her knees part ever so gently as if by some will of their own. Keino's strong masterful hands massaged and stroked each thigh, sending shivers throughout Amara's body. As she shivered, as if on command, Keino gently began to finger her center. He played the essence of her being as though he were a master musician. As he played, providing pulsating pleasure, Amara threw her head back and emitted sounds she had never heard before. With her hands she washed over Keino, feeling every inch of his magnificence. With every touch she was setting fire to his soul. Her hands were pleading with him to enter her secret place. He held on not wanting to end this magical dance. Gently he lifted her body and placed her on the bed. As he laid her body down he worshipped every part of her. He told her in intimate detail how each part of her would soon feel, from the top of her head to the tip of each toe. His words, his touch and his smell, like a fragrant forest, all sent love flowing through her like water down a mountain stream. She was in agony, she felt she could wait no longer. As she writhed beneath him he entered her. The agony became sweet and the pain became pleasure. Her body arched with an urgency she had never known. Keino, with skill and precision, led them soaring unfettered into dimensions not felt on the earthly plane.

Throughout the night they made love repeatedly. With each exploration and subsequent arousal the bond between them was strengthened. Being apart for minutes became unbearable. Their communication often became nonverbal as they spoke with kisses, strokes, electrifying touches, and soulful stares. When Amara awoke the following morning she found Keino sitting in an upholstered chair opposite the bed. He had showered and had a towel wrapped around the lower half of his body, his well formed chest was bare. His eyes peered over steepled hands, his elbows rested on his knees; he looked at her with pure adoration. A flood of memories from the night before cascaded over her as she focused her gaze on his sultry eyes. His tone was laced with the raw act of possession as he said, "Good morning, my sweet, I have been waiting for you. I have been watching you sleep and thinking of the many ways in which I want to please you over and over again for the rest of your life. Amara I want you to be my wife."

As Amara started to respond, Keino rose from the chair and the heat that he emanated suffocated her words. She moved in the bed and for the first time could feel the physical manifestations of the previous night's lovemaking. Every inch of her registered where Keino had left his mark. Intuitively Keino went to her, lifted her from the bed, and walking toward the master bath said, "My darling, I am going to soothe away the aches from our night of pleasure, leaving only ambrosial memories."

With that Amara nestled her head in the hollow of Keino's strong shoulder, and answered, "I will be your wife," while he walked into the bathroom carrying her in his arms like priceless bronze-colored porcelain. Once inside he deposited her on a vanity stool while he prepared a fragrant tub where he soaked, soothed, and suckled her until he surrendered to every fiber of her being. Amara died a thousand deaths. She loved him more deeply with each touch. Tormented, she wanted to love him again and again but Keino, summoning up the control he needed, assured her that they would have much time to partake of the pleasures they had come to crave, but for now her body needed a respite. Amara agreed reluctantly as Keino dried her off like a man obsessed with precious gold.

For the next three days they enjoyed the island together while making plans for their future. They agreed to make the announcement of their upcoming marriage when Keino had taken care of his business in Kenya with the Rono family. Keino was able to expedite his business affairs in Curacao so that he and Amara could swim, snorkel, play, laugh, talk, and eat at the beach. They enjoyed the view of the floating Queen Emma bridge at night lit by hundreds of lights. They took pictures together posed in front of the storybook buildings of Curacao and danced many nights at the island's hot spots. Through it all they loved, and they made love, exploring one another as they had explored the island, with relentless pleasure.

When the time came to leave the island, Kaleb flew them back to Virginia together. They were grateful for the plane ride because it prolonged their parting. Uppermost in Keino's mind was the call he knew he needed to make to his father.

Chapter 21

During the flight home, Amara had the chance to enjoy Keino's brother Kaleb and his antics. It allowed her to see an even more relaxed side of Keino. Kaleb, for the first time in his life, saw a light in his older brother's eyes when he looked at a woman. Yes, he had seen him attracted to women, he had seen him show approval of a pretty face or a well turned ankle, but never had he seen the look he saw when Keino leveled his gaze on Amara. This look spoke of permanence and possession. His brother, he could see, had visited the seat of passion. He could see that Keino was totally swept away by this woman. Kaleb kept smiling to himself, and thought with gleeful anticipation that he could not wait to inform his other siblings. Now they would all know as he did, why Makena held no real interest for Keino. Clearly Keino's soul had found a home elsewhere.

When the plane landed Keino had a driver to take Amara home. He kissed her good-bye and promised to call her later that evening.

As he turned to face his brother they could not help but smile at each other. "So my brother," started Kaleb. "This is the reason Makena cannot get her husband-to-be to the marriage bed. Her husband-to-be wants another in his bed."

"Kaleb, Kaleb, Kaleb always the wise guy," stated Keino playfully. "Is it that obvious?"

"Oh, my brother, wise and serious one, it is so very obvious."

Keino acquiesced, "Yes, Kaleb, I do want to make my life with this woman. My next step is to speak to Father. He needs to pave the way with Makena's family. I am going home in a few days to personally tell Makena's parents what I have told Makena herself more than once."

Kaleb responded, "My brother, I wish you well. Your Amara will be a welcome addition to the family."

When Keino bid his brother farewell and found his way home, his only thoughts were of Amara, the time they had spent together and the future.

As Keino entered the bedroom of his home the house felt emptier than it ever had. He made a mental note to contact Amara's sister, the interior designer. He was sure though, that furnishings alone would not fill the emptiness. He removed his Western attire and exchanged it for a loose fitting, flowing African robe and slippers. He sat in a wingback chair near his bedroom window, picked up his cellular telephone from the nearby nightstand and dialed Amara.

Amara was feeling as though she had floated into her home. She had immediately checked in with her family and her office. Finding that all was well she prepared herself for a luxurious bath. As she bathed, her mind was filled with heated thoughts of Keino. Their adventures together played over and over in her mind. For the first time in her life she knew what it meant to love a man, and she knew her life would be changed forever. Just as she sank into a cloud of bubbles the cordless telephone which she had brought with her into the bathroom rang. She felt Keino's presence before she lifted the receiver. Thoughts of him fluttered like trapped butterflies at the center of her being. When she answered, the sensual thread which had connected them days before came through the sound of his voice and trickled over her. "How are you, my beautiful Amara?" she heard him say.

"Keino, whenever I can hear your voice, I am well."

They both had the urge to seep slowly through the phone wires into each other's arms, instead, Amara kept talking. "I was going to call you to thank you again for my mini-retreat. I really can't remember when I've had a more relaxing time or enjoyed anyone's company so much."

Keino's response was, "We have a lifetime to enjoy. I am going home to Kenya in a few days."

"Oh," was Amara's response.

Keino could hear the hesitation and disappointment in her voice. "My sweet, do not trouble yourself, I will only be gone through the weekend. There is business to which I must attend."

Amara did not ask, but knew that the business to which Keino referred had to do with the elegant cocoa colored beauty and her family. For a brief moment the line was silent, then Keino spoke. "Amara, tonight this house seems very cold and quite empty. Would you like to come over and keep me company? What are you doing at this moment?" he asked.

Amara laughed with the low silken laughter that never failed to arouse Keino. Traces of her laughter remained as she said, "Your timing is so strange, Keino, I'm bathing."

"Ah," said Keino, "I would say my timing is perfect. I will send a car for you in an hour. I'll be waiting."

Before she could answer, he was gone. Smiling to herself and sinking further into the tub Amara started to envision what she'd wear. She opted for black lace undies, black leather pants, a white silk poet's shirt, open at the neck with the collar standing, pearl studs in her ears, a single strand around her neck and ankle high black leather boots to finish off the ensemble. With a spray of Givenchy's Organza and a short leather jacket, she would be ready.

The route to Keino's home was one of the most beautiful in the city. Palatial homes and secluded gated estates lined the roadway. As the car neared his address, the driver slowed and Amara took in the view of Keino's home and the well lit street. Stately evergreens lined the periphery of a magnificent Spanish styled wrought iron fence which enclosed the Mediterranean-styled mansion. The gate was emblazoned with a large M printed in elegant old English script. On one side of the gate was an intercom which the driver used to open the wrought iron masterpiece. Keino was waiting.

He answered the door in all of his splendid African glory. He took her hand, led her into the foyer and began a kiss that lasted until they were both without the ability to do anything other than hold onto each other in a soothing, calming embrace.

"I used to wonder," he said, "why Westerners

were so enthralled with the art of kissing. Now I know."

They both laughed. Amara looked around and said, "Keino, I see you do need my sister's expertise. A little bare," she said, smiling.

Keino continued stroking Amara's back as he responded, "As I said to my brothers, a place to sit, a place to sleep, and electronics—what more do I need?" He stroked the length of her arms as he talked, never able to get enough of the feel of her. As he talked and continued touching her, the thought occurred to him that what he needed to fill his home was Amara and the sounds of the children they were destined to create. Coming out of his reverie he gently kissed Amara again and asked, "May I get something for you? I was about to light a fire and have a glass of port."

"I'd love both," Amara answered. "The fire and the port, those two things will always remind me of the first evening we spent together."

As she spoke the light of love was evident in her eyes. They sipped port and watched the fire, listening to the magnificent sounds of saxophones and trumpets, lying on the Persian rug in front of the fire. Keino took Amara's glass, placed it on the hearth and pulled her close to him. As he stroked her face he said, "Tell me, Amara, do you want children?"

Before she could finish her yes, Keino had covered her mouth with his lips and hungrily started a kiss that moved in energy from her head to her toes. When he moved his mouth from her lips and began to lightly feather her ears, she heard herself repeating, "Yes yes yes."

"How many?" was Keino's question. "How many children do you want?"

"I don't know," was Amara's dreamy response as Keino continued to rain feathery kisses on her throat, ears, and lips.

"How many do you want?" she asked Keino in a dream-like state.

"Twenty," he replied with a straight face. Stunned, Amara jumped and Keino howled with laughter. "My beautiful one, I am only fooling. I look forward to seeing you pregnant with many of my children, but not twenty."

Amara laughed and said, "Thank God. Why don't we just see how it goes. We can start with one."

"Well, maybe," said Keino. "You must know, though, that my father was a twin. None of my other brothers have twins so maybe the ancestors are waiting for us."

"Keino, life with you isn't going to be simple, is it?"

He smiled. "No, my darling. I can assure you it will not be simple, but I can promise you when we marry it will be a good life filled with love and promise."

As had now become their custom they allowed their touching and tasting to ignite their passions until they were lying bare in front of a blazing fire, soul touching soul, riding waves that only they could feel. As the evening cooled and the fire had been reduced to embers, Keino's bedroom became their sanctuary, in which to reignite cravings that could only momentarily be satiated.

Chapter 22

The morning following their passionate night of lovemaking, Keino and Amara had a leisurely breakfast in bed and continued their amorous adventures until early afternoon.

When they could make the day last no longer and evening had fallen, they reluctantly said their farewells. Amara was escorted home by Keino's driver and Keino returned to the emptiness of his home. He felt viscerally the void left without the sight, scent, and feel of the woman he loved. He braced himself for the call he had to make to his father. As thoughts of Amara, long legged, beautiful, and bright, washed over him, he knew a lifetime with her was worth anything he had to endure. His jaw set stoically, looking much like his father when he was determined to get something done, he walked into his cavernous stainless steel kitchen, sat on a black leather–covered bar stool, placed his elbow on the black granite-topped counter, and began to dial the miniature telephone he was carrying in the palm of his hand.

Given the time difference he knew his father would be in his office. Now was the time. As he held the telephone to his ear he could hear the familiar ring. The continental African ring which embodied for Keino a shrillness and distance that was at once disturbing and comforting. Soon a voice came on the line and he heard very distinctive East African tones say, "Mazrui Law Offices."

Keino recognized the receptionist and greeted her with, "Hello, Noni, this is Keino Mazrui. May I please speak with my father?"

"Why, yes, of course, Mr. Mazrui, your father just entered his office. Give him a moment to get settled and I'll ring you through."

"Thank you very much, Noni."

Within a short time The Honorable Garsen Mazrui came on the line. "My son, how are you? It is good to hear from you. Is there some business matter that is pressing?"

Keino smiled inwardly, anticipating his father's propensity to take charge of everything and everyone he touched. There was a slight edge to Keino's voice as he said, "No, Father, this call is about a family matter."

Judge Garsen Mazrui willed himself to freeze, imitating a statue or a palace guard. He froze in his chair, feeling only his heart beating and his lungs expel air as he waited for his son's words. He prayed silently that Keino had made the decision to move forward with his marriage to Makena and remove the strain which was now interfering with normal relations between the Rono and Mazrui families. Judge Mazrui purposely lowered his voice, and moving cautiously into the conversation said, "This sounds very important, my son. What can I do to assist?"

"Father," Keino began, firmly but respectfully, "what you can do is to allow me for a few moments to explain some things to you."

Garsen Mazrui took a deep breath which Keino could hear, and said, "All right, my son, you have my full attention."

"Thank you, Father, I appreciate your indulgence. I will be direct. Concerning my future marriage to Makena, I cannot honor this commitment. I am well aware of the responsibilities inherent in my position in the family. I understand integrity and the importance of family unity, but, Father, I must release Makena so that she can find someone more suitable for her. I know now that I was not meant for Makena."

"Well, my son," the judge spoke quietly and calmly, "This takes me quite by surprise. I have watched for some time as you continually neglected to set a date to take Makena as your bride. I have been puzzled as to what was standing in your way. For that reason I attempted to hasten your decision by giving you a deadline; I see that tact has also failed. Son, have you considered the strain in generational ties? Have you considered our standing in the community? Have you considered the ramifications of this decision on the future of your personal and professional existence?"

Keino replied forcefully, "Father, I have never been a son to take serious matters lightly. If that has not been your experience with me please tell me now so that I can be corrected. I have always honored responsibilities as your eldest son. As a Kenyan I carry the essence of our culture in my very soul. I hold it as close to me as you do, Father, but I will not become a prisoner to it and cut off my lifeline, not just to appease an ancestral tradition. You and Mother gave all of your children a broader world view and with that, the option to live however we choose as morally correct beings. If I am wrong, please, Father, tell me now!"

"Keino," Judge Mazrui said, fighting to maintain his composure, "You know that you are an honorable son. Your mother and I are proud of you and your accomplishments, but this is not a matter we have faced before. A great deal is resting upon the decision you make, and I want to help you think through this situation very carefully. This is one of the most important decisions you will ever make."

Keino replied with a bit of testiness still in his voice, "I am well aware of that, Father."

"What reason are you giving, son? You must have a reason for not marrying Makena."

Quietly, slowly, and with deep conviction Keino replied, "I have found the woman with whom I wish to spend my life."

After a stunned silence Judge Mazrui rushed in with the precision of a surgeon, asking question after question. "Son, when did this happen? How long have you known? Who is her family? Who is she? Does anyone else know?"

Keino had a difficult time controlling his urge to laugh as he heard his father's combination of confusion and hysteria come across the telephone wires. "Slow down, Father, and I will gladly give you every important detail. She is an American of African descent. Her name is Amara Terrell. You met her at the company gala. She is the namesake of Aunt Amara. Her father, Dr. Terrell, was one of the banquet honorees."

As Keino discussed Amara, his mood changed

audibly. Judge Mazrui could hear the awe and longing in his son's voice and his mood lightened as he said, "Oh, yes, yes, a lovely young woman, wonderful family. I see, my son. So the winds of fate have propelled you in another direction? Is your Amara willing to become a part of the life of a man as formidable as yourself?"

"Father, it is Keino Mazrui whom she loves, not my power or my standing in the world, and because of that I want her more than I can say, and she should be my wife. I want to protect her and give her all that I have, always."

After a brief silence, Garsen Mazrui let out a deep breath, slumped in his chair and with deep relief said affectionately to his son, "Keino, when I married your mother it was a break from tradition. Over the years your mother and I have been a formidable team. We have had to be, because the road we've traveled has been difficult. Neither your mother nor I wanted that path to be difficult for our children, but we do understand the meaning of a burning heart. And besides, my son," he said with a warm smile in his voice, "if you had chosen the traditional route you would not be Keino Amare Mazrui. I pray that the two of you will find that you fit so well that the walls of respect and love around you are impenetrable. You will need that protection because as you travel on your marriage journey, there will be many who will not understand, and because of that, will make your days range from challenging to downright traumatic."

"Thank you, Father," was Keino's reply. He was truly relieved and grateful that the first hurdle in his race to marry Amara had been cleared, and he smiled warmly remembering that his mother had said that his father would be on his side. Anxious to move forward, Keino queried, "Father, what should be the next step?"

"Well, son," Garsen Mazrui replied with sartorial command. He was pleased that he and his eldest son were once again moving in the same direction. "the next move will be mine. I will handle the situation with Makena's family. It will not be easy but I have handled situations far more difficult. Though this may not be what Jomo Rono wants, I am certain he will understand and finally accept your decision."

They both laughed as Judge Mazrui said, "Rono's hardest job will be facing his wife."

"Yes, Father, I know," said Keino, still laughing. "And Makena will not be easy for her father either; although her name means happy, I have rarely seen that side of her. Makena has her mother's temperament. Though I have tried to release her from our agreement she has acted as though I've said nothing."

"Never fear, my son, we will find a way to handle this situation so that you can move ahead with your life. Kaleb can fly you home and we can handle this as a family."

"Yes, Father, I have made plans to be home next weekend."

"Good, son, I will alert your mother."

With that, the two men said their good-byes and both sat back to bask in the feeling of relief brought about by the resolution of family dissension.

Chapter 23

NAIROBI, KENYA

As the sun began to set on Nairobi, Judge Garsen Mazrui left his office in the heart of the city's financial district and headed for the opulent suburban area in which he lived. As his chauffeur-driven limousine wheeled through elegantly land-scaped terrain lined by thorn, eucalyptus and acacia trees, Garsen Mazrui continued to think about his conversation earlier in the day with his son Keino, and to outline in his mind the strategy he would use to soothe the ruffled feathers of the Rono family.

As the car pulled into the circular driveway and stopped, the driver opened the door for the judge. Garsen Mazrui breathed a sigh of relief to be home where he looked forward to sharing the day's events with his beloved wife.

As he entered his home he found the house unusually quiet and very peaceful. Customarily it would have been filled with grandchildren or sons or daughters-in-law or friends. Always a hub of activity. He was greeted in the hallway by his long-time houseman, who informed him that his wife, Mrs. Adina Mazrui, was in her sitting room and dinner would be ready for them within the hour.

Judge Mazrui wasted no time making his way to his wife. He found her as enticing and intriguing now as he had when they married. His wife, he knew, was a woman of keen wit, innate compassion and timeless beauty. He rushed to her whenever he could, because he lived to see her love for him shining in her eyes. As he was about to enter the room in which his wife lounged, he stopped at the doorway, giving himself time to take in the serenity personified in his wife. She sat curled up on the sofa, her legs folded beneath her. She was robed in an elegant, fiery red and gold caftan which puddled from the sofa to the floor. Her raven colored hair casually hung on her shoulders. She was engrossed in reading. She felt his presence, looked up and smiled. To his delight the love she felt for him shone in her eyes.

Adina always marveled at the strength and power her husband exuded. His command of his space as he stood or walked, left her with the desire to melt into him, feeling totally and utterly loved and protected. She spoke as he continued to walk into the room. "Welcome home, my husband, how was your day?" She stretched out her hand to meet his as he came closer. When he was close enough to touch her, he sat on the sofa beside her and ever so gently raised her hand to his lips, kissing with feathery wisps each finger and then her palm before returning her hands to her lap. Adina looked at her husband with smoldering eyes and said, "My husband, you always make my soul burn."

Slowly and seductively Garsen replied, "My love, my Adina, it is my desire that you will always burn for me." With a kiss to Adina's cheek Garsen placed himself comfortably on the sofa, loosened his tie, unbuttoned his gray double-breasted suit jacket and placed his feet firmly apart on the thickly padded Turkoman carpet beneath him.

Adina sat watching her husband ritualistically remove from himself the cares of the day. She watched his expression still, and become thoughtfully quiet. She gently touched his shoulder and while she administered long smooth strokes he turned, stared deeply into her eyes, and said with a smile, "Did I hear you ask about my day?"

"Yes, my darling, you did."

As Garsen began to speak, Adina Mazrui thought of how much their love had matured through their years together and she thanked her God and her ancestors for the connection they still felt. As she focused in again on the conversation she heard him say, "Which would you rather do, hear some news which will make you very happy, or help me strategize about resolving the conflict that the good news is going to cause?"

"Oh, my God," responded Adina, "what a way to torture me. You know I will want to know both of those things at the same time."

They both fell into the easy laughter that was their trademark. As the laughter subsided Adina positioned herself in her husband's lap and he began the litany of his day while cradling her like the precious jewel she was to him.

"The most important thing that happened to me today, my darling, was the call I received from our eldest son."

"How is he?"

"Oh, he is well, very well I would surmise from his news," the judge said with a smile in his voice.

"Garsen, stop keeping me in suspense—what news?"

"Well, my lovely one, it seems our son has been smitten by an African American flower."

"Oh, Garsen, how did he sound? Who is she? Oh, I'm so happy for Keino. He has agonized for so long over this issue of finding his mate. The last time he was home I told him it was coming, I could feel it."

"Well, Madam Mazrui, your feelings were correct. He is so taken with this woman I could feel it over the wires."

"Who is she?" Adina inquired.

"My sweet, you fortunately have already met this young woman. Her name is Amara Terrell, your sister's namesake, and also the daughter of the honoree at the Mazrui banquet, Dr. James Terrell."

"You know, Garsen, when I saw them together at the banquet there was something about the way they looked at each other that struck me as different. At the time—with Makena being there and the revelation of Amara's mother having been my sister's college roommate—so much was happening so quickly, I was distracted from really focusing on those two. I remember thinking that she was such a lovely, well bred young woman, and I thoroughly enjoyed her family."

"Well, my dear, if your son has his way we will all soon become family."

"Oh, Garsen, I can feel it. She is the one, she is the one. I know they will do well together. I saw the way our son looked at her and she at him. The fire is there, something I am afraid I never saw in his eyes when he looked at Makena, as lovely as she is. I am so pleased, and now my darling husband, you must work your magic and smooth things over with the Rono family."

"Yes, my darling Adina, and that is where your help will be most appreciated."

"You know I will do whatever is needed, Garsen, and I think I know just where to begin. There is a women's association meeting tomorrow afternoon; I can start to pave the way with Madam Rono before the meeting. I will suggest that we share a meal together. When I smooth the way with her she can begin to prepare her husband for you."

"Adina, as usual, your instincts are perfect. That will work very well. Keino is coming home next weekend, and at that time we will call a meeting with everyone concerned and see if we can't resolve this situation so that our son can marry the woman who has stolen his heart. I will also begin a conversation with Jomo Rono. Amara and Keino will have much to resolve themselves. Just the living arrangements alone in a bicontinental marriage would be enough to dissuade most people. I think those two have the makings of a great team."

"If it can be done, they will do it. And now, my darling, since we are well on the way to resolving one of our biggest family concerns to date, I think we should freshen up for dinner."

As they rose from the sofa to prepare for dinner, Judge Mazrui continued speaking. "I must say, Adina, I was very proud of the way Keino handled our conversation this morning. With all of the respect due me as his father, he let me know in no uncertain terms that he, Keino Mazrui, was not going to go against his heart in this instance for any amount of tradition. He is well aware of our family connections and his responsibilities as the eldest son, and he truly does not want to cause a rift, but he is very willing to fight for what he wants and he wants Miss Amara Terrell." Garsen ended his sentence with a broad smile and an affirmative nod.

Adina looked at her husband, smiled and asked, "Now who does that determined spirit remind you of?"

They both laughed and left the sitting room to prepare to enjoy and intimate dinner for two.

Chapter 24

NAIROBI, KENYA

Obsessing over his sister's delayed marriage was driving Ali Rono literally out of his mind. His mother had taught him, drummed into him all of his life, that he was a Rono. Ali Rono, firstborn son of Jomo Rono. His name and his position in life meant everything. Along with that name came certain responsibilities. Those responsibilities were to be fulfilled. He had already failed to uphold one part of the bargain, for after all, he was also not married. This fact had indeed been a bone of contention with his parents. His mother in particular wanted to brag at association meetings about the trials and joys of grandmotherhood. Twice, suitable marriage arrangements had been made for him and each time a problem arose resulting in no nuptials. He was determined that this would not happen to his sister. The embarrassment, the humiliation, the sorrow, his mother's weeping and moaning. He was not going through it again. No potential suitor would ever reject his sister and live to walk around as if nothing had ever happened. It was common knowledge that his sister Makena Rono was spoiled and willful but Keino Mazrui and his family would not be allowed to rebuff her without paying a price. With the idea of Keino's rejection of his sister fueling his anger, Ali set himself on a dangerous course.

Here he was, Ali Rono in a most unsettling part of Nairobi. A long way from his suburban compound. He was dressed down, clearly below his station in life. Had his mother seen him she would have fainted. He did not want to be recognized, hence the tattered clothing, dark glasses, and a cane rounding out his pretense of blindness. He entered a rundown cubicle passing as a liquor shop. It was empty except for two men who barely acknowledged his presence as he walked to the back of the building to meet the man he hoped would solve all of his problems.

As Ali moved further toward the back of the building he could see an imposing figure leaning on a back wall looking directly at him. He knew the man. This was Avedon, the man he had come to meet. They had known each other as children, though as they grew their social circles were not the same. Avedon had been the son of one of the Rono family servants. A precocious child, Avedon had started engaging in criminal activity at an early age. The criminal activity really began because Ali Rono had taunted him so cruelly about what he did not have as the child of a servant that Avedon had set out to prove that he could get what he wanted, and have what Ali had. And now here they were, with the wealthy Mr. Ali Rono coming to him, Avedon, the felon son of a servant, to beg for a favor. Avedon looked forward with great anticipation to hear Ali plead his case.

The two men acknowledged each other with distant nods and sat at a rickety wooden table in two equally worn chairs. There was no love lost between them. Ali still felt he was Avedon's superior and Avedon felt that Ali Rono was as much of a pompous cowardly fool as he had been when they were children. Ali began. "The precious Mazrui family is rejecting my sister. With all of their wealth and influence the great Judge Garsen Mazrui cannot force his son to fulfill his responsibilities. Something must be done. Keino Mazrui cannot continue to walk the face of this earth if he does not show respect and honor to my family. If he is so callous as to not become a husband to my sister after having her wait all this time, then I want him dead. I will pay you handsomely for ridding us of this problem."

Avedon glared at Ali Rono. He did not move. He thought how correct he had been in his assessment of Ali. Selfish, pompous, cowardly, and surely a fool if he thought any amount of money would entice him to risk his life and a jail sentence for a man who felt that he was so superior to the common man that he could just beckon and he, Avedon, would do his bidding. Ali actually thought that he, Avedon, would take a life for him. Avedon questioned Ali. "Do you really hate the Garsen Mazrui family enough to kill just because Keino Mazrui has been dragging his feet concerning marrying your sister? Have you lost your senses?"

Ali responded furiously. "You imbecile. You don't understand anything. My poor pathetic friend, it isn't just about my sister, my family honor is at stake here. Is my family so insignificant that the Mazruis can just disregard us? Should they be allowed to just keep us on a string waiting for them to pull? Are we so insignificant?" Ali pounded the table and screamed, "Are we?"

Avedon at that moment pitied the man sitting across from him. He started his response slowly, speaking almost as though he were speaking to a child who needed a clear explanation of the realities of life. "I am sure there is an explanation, a reasonable explanation. One which does not require all of this intrigue, not to mention criminal activity. This is a new day, people choose to live differently."

Ali retorted, yelling at the top of his lungs, "You owe me."

Avedon stood, glared down at Ali and with ice in his voice said, "Well, I just paid you with words of wisdom. Consider my debt canceled. I am off the hook. I am finished. If you insist upon completing this lunatic plan you will do so without me. Goodbye, Ali, I'll see you in hell."

Ali fired a string of obscenities at Avedon's retreating back. He slumped in his chair and wept bitterly, the sobbing racked his body. He felt pain as he considered his plight. He had demeaned himself to seek a favor from one he felt was beneath him and he had been left sitting in a slum in a rundown liquor shop weeping like a child. What had he come to? He had to make this right or die trying.

Chapter 25

A lull in her workday found Amara sitting in her office at her desk, basking in the glow of memories of time spent with Keino. She looked forward to seeing him later in the evening. He had said he needed to talk to her about the details of the cancellation of his betrothal. Never in her life had she felt so loved, so adored, so wanted. Thoughts of Keino found her drifting into daydreams of the artistry of his passion-filled kisses. Thoughts of the skill with which he manipulated her body sent her trembling. With her thoughts came a white-hot heat. It scorched her center, and as she swallowed deeply and emitted a tortured moan, the telephone rang. The shrillness of it snapped her back to reality and the desk where she sat. When she remembered that her receptionist was out, she composed herself and picked up the receiver. She answered in the most professional tone she could manage, after her vividly sexual daydream.

"This is Amara Terrell, how may I help you?"

The arrogant Ms. Makena Rono, with haughtiness and contempt in her voice said, "You may help me by not offering yourself as a whore to my future husband."

"Excuse me?" was the stunned response from Amara.

"I won't excuse you. Your behavior is reprehensible. Keino was betrothed to me. He will be my husband no matter how much you throw yourself at him; he will honor his traditions. I know you know nothing of our customs, but Keino knows, and he will not dishonor his family. If you have any respect for yourself you will stay away from him. You could never fit here. Who do you think you are? You American women finding your roots. You have no roots in the Africa in which I live. The rituals and customs which are my birthright have nothing to do with you. Keino's family and my family, the Rono family, have been linked for generations. Our fathers were in the same initiation group. They became men together during the same season. We are locked together by cultural ties as deep as any ocean. For more years than either of us has lived, the Mazruis and Ronos have been locked together. You have no place. I am the chosen one. I was born to be Keino's wife. I was born to give birth to his children. It is expected, and it will be. Our families have been there for each other through every birth, death, marriage, awards ceremony, and business dealings. We have been there for each other! Where were you? You do not belong. Leave Keino alone. He is to be my husband. I am the connection to his ancestors. Leave him alone!"

With that command, Makena hung up. Amara

stared at the receiver momentarily, placed it in the cradle, and then the tears began to flow, softly at first, then a stream, then a flood. Holding herself with both arms wrapped around her breasts she cried and cried, berating herself for ever becoming involved with a man who owed himself to the traditions of another time and place. She kept asking herself, "How could you have been so foolish, so stupid? Sitting here lost in thoughts of a man who can never be yours. Keino isn't free to marry anyone but Makena. He said tonight he wanted to talk, well I will save him the trouble of telling me it was a mistake. No matter what I thought we felt, Keino must know he made a mistake. I will do as Ms. Rono commanded, I will leave him alone." The pain of her decision numbed her. She exhaled, breathing a long sigh, and choked back the remaining tears. As she was looking for Kleenex with which to salvage what was left of her makeup, her sister Cassandra simultaneously knocked and entered her office.

"Hi, sis, no one was at the front desk. Are we still on? It's two o'clock." Cassandra's smile and playful demeanor came to a halt as she looked more closely at her sister's face. "Amara, what's wrong," she said hastily, walking toward her sister. As she got closer she stretched out her arms and Amara fell into them, starting to sob all over again. Cassandra continued holding her sister and said in reassuring tones, "Amara, whatever it is will be all right. Tell me how I can help."

As Cassandra spoke, Amara began to sob as though the world had ended. Cassandra stood her at arm's length and queried her sister. "Amara, what has got you in such a state? Please tell me what's wrong, you know we can fix whatever it is."

The two moved to the small love seat positioned in the corner of Amara's office. They sat across from one another as Amara wept and in between sobs told her sister of the latest developments between her and Keino, explaining his proposal and the vicious telephone call from Makena. While listening and attempting to comfort her sister with an occasional pat on the hand or a stroke on the cheek, Cassandra focused on pulling from herself all of the nurturing energy she could, to bolster her sister's wavering self-confidence.

"Amara, I know the phone call was a shock to your system. It wears me out just hearing about it but, sis, give Keino a chance. From what you told me Makena is old news and she is fighting to stay in a game that is over for her. Look, when I came in here a few minutes ago, one of the things I was so excited about was my meeting with Keino this morning to design the interior of his home. Not only was I taken by what a really great guy he is, but I was really caught off guard by the amount of time he spent talking about your likes and dislikes. If I had not known better, I would have sworn I was decorating for you, not Keino. Every time I asked a question about his preferences, be it color or period pieces, the question out of his mouth was invariably about you. Of course, he tried to question me with all of the skill of a diplomat. He was so transparent trying to get information without giving any. He knew I could see through it, and he didn't care. That man wants you. By the time we finished I knew something was up with you two, and there is no room for Makena."

"But, Cassandra, you don't understand the power of tradition in the Mazrui family, the longstanding ties between Makena's family and Keino's. I think

Keino is fooling himself if he thinks he can go against all of that tradition. I am not going to interfere. I've made enough of a fool of myself putting my heart, my soul, not to mention my body, where they don't belong. As evil as she is, Makena was right."

"You know very well that Makena is as wrong as she can be. You know she is. She is angry because she knows she has lost, and as for Keino, he doesn't strike me as a man who deludes himself. He is clear about the person he wants to spend his days and nights with. If he had wanted Makena, tradition or no tradition, he would have married her already. He wants you, Amara. You had better think long and hard before you throw away the only man who could make you feel the depths of the joy and the pain I've heard you express today. He is your thunder, Amara, hear him. Be available to Keino tonight when he comes, let him explain himself. Then make your decision."

Cassandra hoped that she had said the right words and had comforted her sister. Whether she had or not, she knew she had to call for reinforcements. As soon as she left and went to her home she called Adana and Afiya. If there were words she could not think of, they certainly could.

Chapter 26

When Amara walked into her home that evening, after her tearful discussion with Cassandra, she felt as though part of her life had ended. She dropped her keys near the front door and walked straight back to her kitchen. The last remnants of sunlight were streaming through the multi-windowed space. At other times this spacious kitchen with its warm yellows, the colors of jonquils and daffodils in bloom, made her happy. It always filled her with a sense of completeness and contentment.

Today was different. Leaning against the nutmeg colored, granite-topped counter she welcomed the coolness of its surface as she placed her hands palms down, hung her head and took deep cleansing breaths to calm the mixture of anger and deep sadness that permeated her body. In one hour she would have to face Keino. How was she going to face him? She did not know, but she had to face him one last time to end what they had only begun. Makena, however malicious, was right. She, Amara, did not belong in Keino's world.

The prospect of giving up the only man she had ever loved was more painful for Amara than anything she had ever endured. With the thought of ending her relationship with Keino pounding in her head, the air around her became thick and heavy, laden with pain and sorrow. Once again she sat and wept.

Her sisters' calls, each in turn, gave her time to reel in her spinning emotions and try to ready herself for her confrontation with Keino. She had to smile through fading tears when she thought of Adana the lawyer, telling her that with just a word from her, she would sue Ms. Makena for slander and she promised it would be a court battle Makena would never forget.

Afiya offered words of wisdom from her favorite West African philosopher Malidoma Some'. She reminded Amara that according to Some' the spirit and the mind are one and that she should not deny what her heart said, calling it impossible. She should run with all her might toward new possibilities.

Her sisters were so different yet all three equally wise. Right now she had to pull from her own reservoirs of wisdom. She prayed that she could.

Keino was ending an extremely busy workday. His calendar had been filled, but Amara had never been far from his thoughts. As visions of her streamed through his consciousness, he was possessed by an overwhelming desire to protect her from anything that interfered with the passion they shared. She was a strong, independent woman whom the Creator had fashioned as a perfect fit for him. He was grateful that his parents understood and would stand with him as he proclaimed to the Ronos—and the world—that Amara would be his wife. He smiled soulfully with the corners of his mouth lifting and light shimmering in his eyes. He picked up his briefcase and headed for his sleek sedan to drive to Amara's home. He could not wait to tell her that all was well with his father.

On the drive to Amara's, Keino's only thoughts were of making love repeatedly to the woman he wanted more than life. Seeing her, being with her, gave him a sense of peace that only came with her touch. He wanted their bodies and souls to merge and never part. He wanted Amara in every way he could want a woman. As he drove into her driveway, a sudden uneasiness fell over him. The house seemed unusually quiet and almost dark. Only a dim light radiated from the house. He parked, got out of the car and walked briskly up the flower lined pathway to the front door. Reaching the door he pushed the doorbell and waited for a response. As he stood, legs apart and hands clasped behind his back, his sense of uneasiness mounted. He pushed the doorbell a second time and waited impatiently for a response. Just as he lifted his hand to pound the door, it opened. The woman standing in the doorway was a shadow of the woman he loved. The perpetual light in her eyes was gone, in its place was a dark vacantness, and the lifelessness in her body replaced the welcoming loving spirit she had always reserved for him. Fueled by the sense of uneasiness he was feeling and the suspense of wondering what had happened to Amara, Keino willed himself still. The smile which earlier had radiated from his face was now a distant memory. As he looked at Amara what she saw were cold questioning eyes as he asked calmly, "Amara, why is the house almost dark? Why did you not answer the door? What is wrong?" As he looked at her, there was a distance in Amara's eyes that Keino did not recognize. It chilled him as he tried to read her face. He walked through the door, closed it behind him and reached for her; as he did she stepped away and walked into her dimly lit living room and sat on the sofa. She watched as though watching a stranger as he moved in the room. He lifted an accent chair, and positioning himself in front of Amara, sat down, legs wide, elbows placed on his knees, with intense eyes peering over steepled hands covering lips which whispered a pleading, "Amara, please tell me what is wrong. I come to you and find you sitting in a house with barely any light, you almost refuse to answer the door and when you do, you do not speak to me. I try to touch you and you turn away. I am looking at a woman whose lifeless body I scarcely recognize. Please, my darling, tell me what is wrong."

Amara, emotionally weakened by the events of the day, knowing that she had to walk away from a love that she had only dreamed about, could not stop the flood of tears that came. As her body shook with sobbing, Keino rushed to her side, cradled her in his arms and pleaded with her to tell him what was tormenting her. As Amara was able to bring her tears under control she moved away from Keino and in barely audible tones said, "Keino, please just let me say what I need to say without touching me. I can't think clearly if you touch me. Right now I hurt so much."

Wanting to absorb her pain, Keino reached for Amara while she continued to say, "Keino, please, no, I need to do this my way. Just please let me finish what I need to say." Keino eased back and allowed Amara the space to express her pain, her rage and her sadness.

"Keino, we both know that I have never loved anyone in the way that I love you. I have given you my heart, my soul, my body. We have shared in ways I have never experienced. I knew when I got involved with you, who you were. I told myself I could enjoy your company and when the time came I could walk away; and then you asked me to marry you and I thought my prayers had been answered. I thought we could just get married, and live our lives. I didn't understand the power of centuries old African traditions. I had no idea. I don't fit. I can't marry you and make your life miserable, damage your personal and professional standing in the community that matters most to you. You know we can't be married. For the sake of your family name we can't be married."

Keino was stunned, but only he knew the depth of the pain he was feeling as he sat looking at, and listening to, Amara. He vowed he would not allow his emotions to take over and throw him into a fit of rage. He vowed silently to stay calm and get to the bottom of this devastating decision Amara had made.

He positioned himself firmly once again in the chair and said with heart-wrenching emotion, "My darling, as surely as there are stars in the heavens you will be my wife. You are the one woman on earth for whom I was born. You are for me, Amara. You are my life's blood, you carry the womb from which my children shall come. You are me, you are my woman. I will never leave you and I will never let you go. If I cannot have you I will have no one."

With clouded eyes Amara pleaded, "Keino,

please just honor your tradition. I will not be the reason you are ostracized by the Ronos and countless others. Makena may be mean but she was right about that."

Keino's eyes froze as he asked, "When did you speak with Makena?"

Amara blinked, cast her eyes down as though in thought, looked at Keino for a long moment and said, "I am sorry my love. I didn't intend to tell you that she called me today, and told me to stop offering myself as a whore to her future husband."

Amara had never seen such fury in Keino's eyes. His voice was low and deep as he said, "Now I understand your behavior. Makena is not the woman I want. She is not the woman I have ever wanted. It is true traditions and customs as old as time are revered in my country, but everything evolves with the passage of time. I remember telling you before, and I am telling you now that my family will handle this situation. Arrangements have been made for an end to all of this nonsense next weekend." Keino drew in a sharp breath. His eyes darkened as he said, "You, my love, are to be my wife. The only people now who need to give us their blessings when I return from Kenya, are your parents. I need nothing from the Ronos or anyone else. What I need is you, Amara, you."

He continued to speak. "Amara, from the moment I saw you, the path to my destiny was opened to me. For all of her talk about tradition, Makena does not understand me, nor does she understand my parents. My parents want what is best for their children regardless of tradition. All they ever ask is that we handle things respectfully. For that reason, Amara, I am going home to go through the protocol of facing Makena's parents to tell them in person that their daughter is not suited for me. You must understand, my darling, I am not jeoparding anything, not my future, not my family name, not my standing in the community, nothing! I have spoken with both my parents. They are very clear that I want you to be my wife for as long as I live. They are happy for me, for us." His face lightened as he smiled and said, "Even Kaleb thinks I've made the right choice. So you see, my darling, we have nothing to fear. Our future together is bright. Ten thousand Makenas and all the Ronos in the world cannot stop what we have begun."

As Keino explained away Amara's fears, she knew with an assurance and a certainty that she had never felt before that she was to be Mrs. Keino Mazrui.

Breath caught in Amara's throat as she saw the fire of rage in Keino's eyes turn to the smoldering heat of need and desire. Her pulse raced. She felt her body warm to a sensuous glow as she felt Keino lift her off her feet, cradle her in his arms and kiss her deeply and reverently. Still holding her, he started walking toward the staircase. In that moment he remembered that he had no knowledge of the layout of her home. He whispered softly, "Tell me the way to your bedroom."

With her face nuzzled in the hollow of Keino's powerfully built neck, Amara answered, caught in the throes of a raw primal heat, "The first door on the right of the staircase."

Keino slowly walked up the stairs, professing his love for Amara. When he found the bedroom door, he carried Amara into her semi-darkened room. Diffused rays of the dim lighting from downstairs cast a shadowy haze allowing Keino to see the outline of the bed. He laid her gently down

on the smooth silken comforter and turned to
find a lamp on a side table. He turned it on. It
emitted a perfect glow of amber lighting. He sat
on the bed beside Amara and while telling her of
her beauty and his love for her, he began removing her clothing slowly and seductively, piece by
piece, until she could feel the coolness of the
silken comforter contrasting the smoldering heat
which was now her body. Keino marveled at how
any one woman, his woman, could be so exquisitely formed. As if in worship, Keino lifted one of
Amara's long golden arms above her head and
began to lavish long lazy strokes from her fingertips down the long smooth plane which ended at
her inner thigh. He stroked and kissed, alternating
sides, worshipping at the shrine of Amara until she
felt she would be driven out of her mind by Keino's
divine ministrations. When she felt she could take
no more he began to kiss and suckle each of her
taut satiny nipples. Aching, Amara pleaded for Keino
to make love to her. Keino ignored her pleas and
continued long lingering strokes and deep hungry
kisses, eliciting turbulent waves of electricity
throughout Amara's very soul. Her quivering, soft
velvety lips and writhing body took Keino to maddening heights. His body instinctively hardened
with each movement that Amara made. The air
around them closed in, shrouding them in mixtures
of sweet perfume and the bitter tantalizing smells
of raw passion. Amara began to tear at Keino's clothing. When she was unable to free him from the re-
strictions of his garments, he stilled her hands with
his own, lifted her hands, kissed each finger, and
began with all of the control and concentration of
a warrior king to disrobe. Amara watched Keino's
powerfully built body as each ripple of muscle re-

acted to the elegance with which he moved. The same hands which had set her on fire were now preparing to unleash even more of the exquisite ecstasy that only Keino could provide. Keino willed himself not to allow desperation and extreme need to overtake him. He wanted to brand Amara with the depth of his feelings, he wanted her to succumb to his ways of pleasuring her, cementing them together for a lifetime.

As he removed his clothing, Keino fixed his gaze on Amara and the two were locked silently in a dance of unspoken passion awaiting an intoxicating release. He moved with power and grace and eased in beside her on the bed. The fires which had been embers now threatened to blaze out of control. Keino and Amara urgently began their explorations of one another. It felt impossible to satiate their need and longing. Keino, with precision and mastery, repeatedly aroused and tantalized Amara until she was sure her cries of delight were heard worlds away. She was tortured sweetly with every touch, stroke, and kiss. Keino transported her to places only he could take her. In turn, her soft pliable hands burned him as she touched and stroked him. Her cries of pleasure at the feel of his powerfully hard body sent his heart thundering as he savored her. He wanted the torment they called pleasure to be prolonged. Amara's soft ravenous pleading left him ready to devour her. With ferocious intent he captured her mouth and with slow, drugging kisses he imitated the intimacy that they had shared during their nights and days of loving. He pressed her to him and took her mouth over and over again with a dominating intensity. She drank in his hunger, his desperation, his passion, his love. He left her mouth and as she stroked his long muscular back he kissed repeatedly her silken belly and then he traveled from belly to cottony soft thigh, leaving her weak and burning. As he made music at the center of her being, she shattered. Her soul scattered throughout the universe. Her reentry was sweet; Keino's smiling face was there to greet her as the pure joy of being loved well shone on her face. Keino, with a smile and sense of joyous power, eased himself up to cradle Amara in his arms. At that moment she became conscious of his arousal and as his hands roamed intimately over her swollen breast she moaned softly and slipped her hands around his glorious manhood. He took a deep breath, and as she arched up to meet him he slipped into her and they flew to paradise.

Chapter 27

NAIROBI, KENYA

The Kenyan sun was shining brightly, heralding a new day of promise and mystery. Keino was home again, awaiting the meeting of the Ronos and the Mazruis. The meeting was to finally settle ancient matters so that he and Amara would be able to move freely and fully into the future. He was pleased that he and Amara had cleared a major misunderstanding.

Sitting in the library of his family home, Keino sat with his head cradled in his hands massaging his temples, attempting to wash away his conflicting feelings of obligations to the old ways while living and operating in a thoroughly modern world. He knew he had to speak to Makena before the meeting but he wanted to dampen the anger he felt toward her because of her call to Amara. It would do no good at this point to antagonize Makena—that would only serve to prolong this ancient dance they were all doing. He knew he had to call her to pave the way for civilized communication. Keino looked at the telephone positioned on a nearby desk. Though he felt the attempt would be futile, he knew he had to give Makena a final opportunity to save face for herself and her family and release them both from the betrothal. He picked up the receiver and dialed Makena's private line. She answered on the second ring.

"Makena, it is good to hear your voice. I hope that you are well—"

Before Keino could finish his insincere salutation, Makena cut in. "Keino, let's dispense with the pleasantries that you don't mean. All of the pleasantries in the world won't make it easier for me to accept that our wedding has been canceled."

"Makena," he began slowly, reining in his anger, "you knew, you have known, that I have no desire for us to be married. It would be a sham, a pretense. Don't pretend that this is all news to you. The act that you are putting on for your family and friends may fool some, but you know that we both know the truth of the situation."

Makena rushed in, feigning contrition. Not used to not having her wishes obeyed, she decided that she would try one last time to convince Keino to see things her way. "But, Keino, we deserve a chance, we'd have a great life. I was made for you. Our lives have been connected since our youth. The culture you love so much, I am a part of, I could transmit it to our children. Why are you throwing it all away on some American who has not a clue as to who you are and what your life demands? It is a waste, Keino, to renounce centuries of traditions for an American. What are you doing?"

Keino began with patient tones which covered his seething anger.

"First of all, Makena, Amara has nothing to do with my decision not to marry you. We both know our marriage would be a disaster. Just sharing a culture is not enough to build a life. Makena, I'm asking you one last time to agree to release us both from this tie so that our families can go on with their lives in peace."

Makena in strident tones reiterated, "Keino, I don't care what you want. I know we should be married. I am not going to make it easy for you. If you want to be rid of me you will have to do it publicly in front of our parents. You can embarrass yourself by going against tradition; I will not make it easy for you."

Keino spoke with resignation in his voice. "All right, Makena, have it your way. We will all go through this ritual so that you can once again be the center of attention. Fine. I will gladly make it known to your family that I do not now, nor have I ever, wanted you as my wife." Keino placed the telephone in its cradle and Makena was left fuming on the other end. Keino looked around the room in which he sat, and viewed with a critical eye the setting that was the home in which he had been reared. He examined the opulence, the comfort, and the modern conveniences, and almost laughed at the thought of having to be subjected to rituals that dated back hundreds of years. He regretted having to put his parents through the ordeal of facing the Ronos. He knew what theatrical events these negotiations could be, but he also knew that he was willing to walk through fire to live his life with Amara. As he unfolded himself from the plush leather chair in which he sat, and rose to his full height, he knew he was ready. In the moment in which he stood, all angst and uncertainty fell from him. With purposeful strides, and the royal carriage that was second nature to him, Keino headed in the direction of the drawing room where he knew his parents would be waiting.

As he entered the elegant room, his parents were deeply engaged in what appeared to be a most intimate exchange. He knew instinctively that they were strategizing about the day's upcoming proceedings.

Keino's mother was the first to speak as he entered the room. "Hello, my son," she said, greeting him with her usual affectionate kiss and embrace. "How are you feeling?" she queried. "Have you recovered from your transcontinental flight?"

"Yes, Mother, I am fine," Keino said, returning his mother's embrace. "I am anxious to get to the Ronos to clear everything up so that I can move on with my life."

At that moment Judge Mazrui, in a reassuring gesture, rose and placed his hand on Keino's shoulder and said with sartorial splendor and command, "My son, nothing will deter us today. Our battle is already won. Now, are you ready?"

Keino answered, "Yes, Father! I am ready." He thought of Amara and said with an upturned smile, "I have a woman to marry and children to produce."

With that glint of humor, all of them laughed aloud. Judge Mazrui, returning to his more serious nature, spoke. "I am happy that we can find some humor in this comedy of errors. Now, my son, when we are seated in the Rono home, Jomo and I will begin the traditional banter. When your turn comes, I have but one request of you, my son, show some remorse. Please allow the Ronos to save face, as it were. We want to salvage what we can of the generational family ties which we share."

"Father, I will do my best. It is not my intention to damage family relationships, I just want a settlement of this matter that is equitable for everyone."

"Your mother and I have both spoken to the Ronos separately. Jomo, Makena's father, seemed more open to discussion than her mother Apiyo, but she must adhere to the decision of her husband. God knows he has her input, and he must do what he thinks is best for his family, as I must do what is best for mine. I am concerned about Jomo's son Ali. He is such a hothead and his arrogance will be the death of him. I hope his father can reel him in. Well, it will be what it will be. The time has come. Our driver is waiting." Garsen Mazrui switched into the demeanor of a man about to put his world in order.

Keino and his parents walked to the waiting Mercedes limousine, entered, seated themselves, and rode in pensive silence to the Rono property minutes away from their own estate.

The beauty of the day was in direct contrast to the mood which prevailed in the Rono household as the Ronos awaited the arrival of the Mazruis. Jomo Rono, the head of the Rono family, sat statue-like, awaiting the arrival of his lifelong friend Garsen Mazrui. The occasion was not joyful as others had been, but he nevertheless welcomed the opportunity to resolve the matter of the delayed marriage of their betrothed offspring. Sitting in his frozen state he perused his parlor like the hawk he so admired. He found the creature formidable in appearance and yet the bird embodied for Jomo the personification of wisdom. Hawks always appeared to him to be creatures that weighed every action, and seemed to execute their functions with precision and deliberation. In all of his dealings, whether personal or business, Jomo saw himself as a hawk. Today he prayed that God and his ancestors would intervene in this situation and infuse him with the wisdom he so admired and wished to embody. Jomo had suffered a tormented sleepless night and his morning had been no better. His wife Apiyo had been insisting for days that he stem the tide of progress and change the mind of Keino Mazrui and somehow force him to marry their daughter Makena. He was not God and he knew that only God and the ancestors could turn this situation around. God and the ancestral powers had been consulted and the change had not come. He could hear Apiyo and her children in the next room, yelling at the tops of their voices about whose fault it was that Keino Mazrui had not chosen to honor his marriage commitment. Truthfully, he, Jomo Romo, could not blame Keino. Keino had become a fine young man, and sadly, both of his children, from his first wife Apiyo, were willful, arrogant, and spoiled. He loved them because they were his children, but he could certainly see why suitable mates were not clamoring at their doors. He felt sorry for his children because their mother had reared them to believe that everyone owed them, and he had sat by and watched it happen. He had hoped that today they could all put this fiasco behind them and move forward with some dignity, but he could see that his wife was going to make things difficult. She wanted her pound of flesh. Poor Apiyo; she always wanted more. She never felt she was enough or that he was enough. More, more, more, was her constant mantra. Her children had inherited the same insidious disease.

As he heard what he thought to be a car pull into the driveway, he knew the time had come to settle the matter which had torn up his household for months. He walked to the room adjoining the one he occupied, swung open the door with a force that startled the occupants, his wife and children, and as they turned to look in his direction, he raised his large hand in a signal to stop. He gritted his teeth and with a thundering voice, which demanded compliance, he said with features set in a way that were deceptively composed, "This house will now become quiet. Our guests are arriving. You will conduct yourselves with dignity. I will not be left to be ashamed of your behavior."

Apiyo was the first to comply. She pulled herself to her feet, smoothed down the fabric of her traditional gown, touched her gelee to make sure of its position on her head, and looked at her husband with cold angry eyes and walked past him into their sitting room to await those she had once revered as friends. Makena followed, as beautiful and as haughty as ever. Her graceful glide would have shamed most runway models. She had chosen Western attire for the occasion, and the off-shoulder white-jade sheath with matching mules accentuated every positive physical feature Makena had, from her long neck and well defined clavicles to her minuscule waist and perfectly rounded hips leading to long, slender, perfectly formed, cocoa colored legs.

Makena was enjoying this game, all of this fuss over her. She truly loved being the center of attention. She pitied her poor mother and brother who were seemingly going mad over her future. It would have been laughable had they not been so serious. She continued to play the game. She loved making each of them weep as she played her role as the rejected one. She knew, too, that her fawning and playing the dejected princess had really affected her father. He had always just given her whatever she wanted not to hear her complain. He couldn't do it this time so she harped and complained more loudly and she loved every minute of seeing him become agitated and endlessly frustrated with her shedding tears that only she knew were false. And her brother was the most gullible of all. Ali could be manipulated to do anything for her. She smiled as she looked across the room at him and thought of his stupidity. Ali caught her eye as she was smiling, and felt even more determined to avenge his sister's rejection. He knew his father could be placated by anything the Mazruis told him. Well he, Ali Rono, would not allow his family to be subservient to the Mazruis. At that moment he was sure of what he must do.

The Rono family took their seats in their living room. It was a room like Madam Rono, filled with many luxuries and little taste. The elder Ronos sat side by side in two French provincial chairs resembling thrones. Makena and Ali sat on ornate settees placed on either side of their parents. The Ronos waited in grim silence as the Mazruis stepped from their car, and walked to the Ronos' front door. The Rono family houseman opened the door for the Mazruis and announced their arrival as he had been instructed. Jomo stood and Garsen Mazrui walked forward towards him with an outstretched hand which Jomo shook. The air in the room was solemn as the Mazruis took their seats. Garsen

Mazrui began. "Rono family, I am very grateful that we have been granted this time to speak, and to mend fences. Our history together is long and productive, we have created much goodwill over time. It is our hope, that of the Mazrui family that the goodwill continues, and that our families will always be connected. We know that times are changing and many of the old ways are slipping away. Even in our generation there were those of us who chose a different path. I beg your indulgence for my son to make a different choice. We also wish you to understand that his decision is not a reflection of the beauty, the intelligence, or the worthiness of your daughter. We wish her well and will help her to achieve any of her future endeavors."

Garsen Mazrui had paved the way, now it was Keino's turn. Keino's heart was pounding. He wanted to curse this tradition and all of its meaningless ceremony. He didn't want that spoiled brat Makena, and he knew she didn't really want him, not as the man he was. She didn't even know the man he was. He wanted to tell them all that he was leaving, and that he was marrying Amara and that he wanted them to stay the hell away from his new bride. Instead he began slowly and calmly, "Mr. Rono, Madam Rono, I have known you both since I was a child. I intend to cause your family no harm and I mean no disrespect. You know me. You know my family. We have never before done anything to deliberately offend you, and so I ask your indulgence as I formally release Makena from our betrothal."

Apiyo could not wait for her husband's response. "Keino, dear Keino, let's not be hasty, you must not be thinking clearly. Sometimes things happen to push us off course. Perhaps you are just off course right now, but we know that Makena is the wife for you. She knows your ways. She knows your traditions. She will make a mother of which your children could be proud. She was bred for a man of your station."

At that moment an embarrassed Jomo looked directly at his wife, took her hands in his and spoke. "Forgive my wife, she is overwrought with these matters. Apiyo finds it difficult to let go when her children are involved."

Ali Rono was boiling. How dare his father apologize to these people for his mother. The Mazruis should apologize to the Ronos. He jumped to his feet and entered the conversation, superseding his father's authority. He yelled frantically, "We are not the ones who should apologize. Father, the Mazrui family has treated us like servants. They have ignored tradition, they have slapped us in the face. We have been disgraced. My sister has been rejected by this avaricious playboy. He should pay."

The room was shocked into silence. Jomo was first to speak. Feeling raging anger and a sense of his fading power, he spoke with a distant coldness in his voice. "Once again my family has lost its sense of control. Traditions are being disregarded in more than one way today. Keino, regardless of what my son and my wife feel, I understand your right to have your point of view." Still trying to hold on to his authority as the head of his family, Jomo looked pointedly at his wife and children and said, "We will hear Keino out, and we will not express our displeasure in a dishonorable way. There is but one person in the Rono family who has in this instance the right to offer respectful objections to the proceedings."

In a louder voice this time, Jomo said, "Makena

is the only one of us who has much at stake and she has not spoken, though people have spoken for her. I think it is Makena whom we should hear." Jomo focused his attention on his beautiful daughter. She sat looking so delicate and so serene. He hoped she would now bring some civility to this ceremonial ritual gone awry. Makena uncrossed her lovely legs, stood behind her mother and started a tirade for which her father, and the rest of those present, were totally unprepared. She addressed Keino.

"I, Makena Rono, do not need to have my family beg for your acceptance of me as your wife. You don't deserve me, Keino Mazrui. I am too good for you, and your family. I am now, and I have always been. You deserve the whore you have chosen."

Makena's father and mother and Garsen and Adina Mazrui were so shocked they were frozen to their seats. This was a Makena none of them had seen. Keino, not at all surprised that Makena had taken off her mask and revealed the maliciousness she was capable of, threw his head back, and laughed out loud. His laughter was the container for the anger he wanted to unleash on Makena. He moved in front of her so quickly she did not see him coming. He stood in her face, and with a diabolical smile which caused Makena to freeze said, "Makena Rono, I know you better than you know yourself. You may say whatever you like to me, but if you ever again call my future bride a whore you will live to regret it."

Jomo knew he had lost total control. Before he could reprimand his daughter, his son, as if from out of nowhere, jumped in front of Keino, pointing a pistol at Keino's head, yelling, "How dare you speak to my sister in that manner, in that tone." His voice became louder with each word until he was screaming, "Who do you think you are? Where do you get the authority to order lives in the way that you want? You are not God, you are just a Mazrui and I am going to end that right now."

As Ali waved the pistol, Keino read the madness in his eyes and knew that he had a split second to save his own life. With the speed and agility of a cat he lunged at Ali, and grabbed at the gun. As Keino wrestled Ali to get the gun from him, the gun fired. The minutes that elapsed felt like hours as the room and it occupants stilled, watching the two men locked in a death-defying struggle. The gun fired again. Both men froze. Wildly beating hearts made the only audible sound. Ali fell to the floor like a rag doll. The gun left his hand and skidded across the room. Blood splattered everywhere. Apiyo screamed and cried, yelling, "My son is dead. Oh, my God, my son is dead."

Adina Mazrui, who had remained quiet throughout the meeting, tried to comfort Apiyo while Jomo, Keino, and Garsen took care of getting the wounded Ali to emergency medical services and alerting the police. Makena stood frozen in place, as still as her brother. She was no longer the center of attention.

Chapter 28

The Mazruis and the Ronos minus Makena, sat in the emergency waiting room of Meru Hospital, one of the finest hospitals in Nairobi, waiting as a team of surgeons with international reputations worked to save Ali's life.

The Ronos and Mazruis had been questioned by the police and it appeared quite clear that Ali, if he survived, was to be charged with attempted murder. Ali's mother was devastated, his father was saddened by the loss of the son he thought he had known. Garsen and Adina Mazrui were sad for the Ronos, but were grateful to God and their ancestors that Keino's life had been spared.

Adina Mazrui continued to walk and talk with Apiyo. Madam Rono was almost inconsolable at the thought of her son's demise. Madam Mazrui tried to assure her that Ali had the finest doctors and that they were doing their very best to save his life. Neither of them could speak about the possible prison sentence that lay ahead of him. Keino, his father, and Ali's father sat silently, stoically, each knowing that Ali had brought about his own death, if it should come to that. In his silence, Jomo sat blaming himself for not paying closer attention to the madness developing in his son. Obsessed by his own life and work, he had missed the cues that would have alerted him to his son's obsessive behavior. He would never forgive himself for this very costly mistake.

Garsen Mazrui sat feeling sad for his old friend, and for all of them. He marveled at how traditions designed to bring cohesion and unity could sometimes cause such division and anger. In the midst of all of the sorrow surrounding him he was proud that his son had chosen to stand his ground for a life of his choice just as he, Garsen, had done in his youth. He began silently praying for Ali Rono's family.

Keino sat astounded that in a split second his life could have been lost. He felt for Ali. The poor soul had become obsessed with lives and circumstances that he could not control. All of that anger for a sister who thought less of him than she would a pet dog. She had not even had the decency to come to the hospital. He felt sad for them all but he knew that his life had been spared to share with Amara, the woman sent from the heavens for him and only him. He knew he had to call her soon. She would be waiting for news of the family meeting. As he looked at his watch to calculate the time difference, he saw the chief surgeon coming toward them. Keino stood, as did Garsen and Jomo. Keino tried to read the look in the surgeon's eyes, but he was unable to gauge the practiced inscrutable look the surgeon wore. By the time the doctor reached the area where the three men were sitting, Adina and Apiyo, who were headed in that direction, upon seeing the doctor picked up their pace. They reached the gathering just as the chief surgeon started to speak.

"After four hours of surgery we were able to save Ali's life, but the bullet entered his body in such a way that he suffered paralysis of both his legs. It is doubtful that he will ever walk again."

Hearing the doctor's words, Apiyo fell into her husband's arms and wept a profusion of bitter tears. Keino said his good-byes to his parents and left them while they consoled the Ronos. He hurried back to his parents' home to call Amara. He needed to hear her voice, he needed to reassure her that though the meeting had been a disaster, his love and need for her were intact, and that they would go on with their lives.

When he entered his parents' home, for the first time that day he was able to breathe a sigh of relief. Walking into the cocoon of his family home strengthened and calmed him. What happened at the meeting was well beyond anything he could have imagined. Everyone knew that Ali was an impassioned man, a man with great zeal and immense loyalty when it came to family, but this time he had gone beyond the limits of civilized life. The consequences were immense. Not only was he paralyzed, but he would certainly be jailed for attempted murder.

As the disbelief of the day's events washed through his mind, Keino mounted the stairs of his familial residence to the room he occupied when visiting. He simultaneously entered the room and started removing the garments he wore, which had been painted with Ali's blood. He entered his adjoining bath, turned on the shower full force, and stepped into a glass enclosed waterfall. He lathered his skin furiously, washing away, for him, the remains of an ancient tradition, which had ended in modern day destruction, and devastation. He stepped out of the shower, dried himself off, and dressed in one of his many traditional African robes. He sat on his bed, propped his well-developed torso against the padded headboard, and stretched his long legs in front of him. He reached for the telephone on the nightstand, and dialed Amara. He hoped to find her at home. Since Nairobi was eight hours ahead, he thought he might speak with her before she left for her office. His timing was perfect. Amara answered on the first ring, anticipating Keino's call.

"Hello," she said in quiet tones, hoping that Keino's voice was on the other end.

"Hello, my darling, how are you?" As Keino spoke he could feel his desire for her rise as he envisioned her holding the receiver.

"Oh, Keino, I've been so worried about you, about the meeting. I've been procrastinating leaving for the office; I didn't want to leave the house until I had heard from you. How are you? How did the meeting go?"

"Amara, I want you to sit down and brace yourself for quite a story."

Fear shook Amara; her thoughts ran uncontrolled. What could have happened that she needed to sit? She released a volley of questions: "Why do I need to sit down, Keino? Oh, my God, did something happen? Oh, Keino are you all right?"

She could hear the stillness and the seriousness in Keino's voice as he said, "Are you sitting, Amara?"

Sensing that Keino needed steadiness from her now and not panic, "Yes," was her quiet reply.

Keino then began to recount the events of the day. When he was finished Amara was weeping tears of sadness at the destruction of life, and tears of joy and thanksgiving that Keino's life had been spared. If she hadn't known before, she surely knew now, that she would never give Keino up, for had he died, her world would have ended.

They agreed that when he returned to Virginia he would speak to her parents about their desire to be married and they would then begin a blissful journey together.

Chapter 29

When Keino and Amara walked into the home of Drs. Ana and James Terrell, Amara and Keino saw the smiling welcoming faces of Amara's parents, and sisters. The smiles said that everyone present knew that Amara had called this family meeting to make a joyous announcement. Amara's father was the first to speak. While speaking to Keino, he wrapped his daughter in a loving embrace. A warmth echoed in his voice as he said, "Good to see you again, Keino."

Keino replied with a broad smile and an outstretched hand, "And you, Dr. Terrell. It is great to see you."

Ana's greeting was an embrace for both her daughter and Keino. Pleasantries were passed all around as Amara's sisters lovingly greeted their sister and the man they knew to be the love of her life. Amara's mother suggested that they all move into the family room, to continue their conversation. Ana was thrilled by the prospect of what she felt in her heart was the announcement of an upcoming marriage between her daughter Amara and the elegant Mr. Keino Mazrui. The way they looked at one another, and Keino's protective demeanor around Amara let Ana know that much had transpired between the two since she had last seen Mr. Keino Mazrui.

Everyone moved into the large cozy family room and seated themselves comfortably. An air of joyous anticipation filled the room.

Once they were seated Keino took Amara's hand and started to speak in deep purposeful tones. He began as he had been taught, in the traditions of both his parents, by addressing Amara's entire family. "Dr. and Mrs. Terrell, Adana, Cassandra, and Afiya. From the moment Amara shook my hand, my spirit knew that she should be my wife. In the beginning I denied my own heart, because of antiquated tradition and silly stereotypical thinking; but what I feel for your daughter, and your sister, I have never felt in my life and I am certain I will never feel again." At that moment Keino's eyes met Amara's, and locked in a silent communication reserved only for lovers. After a moment he continued speaking. "With your permission I would like to ask for Amara's hand in marriage. Our families will become one, and I will love and protect Amara until the day I die."

Dr. James Terrell glanced around the room after Keino finished speaking and saw all of the women in the room misty-eyed. With a smile in his voice and deep respect for Keino in his soul James said, "Son, it would be our privilege to welcome you to this family."

Feeling an overwhelming sense of joy, Amara's

mother and her sisters embraced one another, laughing and crying as they threw out questions and suggestions about wedding dates, times, and places. They were happy to be of service to plan a wedding fit for royalty. Keino and Dr. Terrell looked at the women, then at each other, shook their heads, and walked laughing like old companions into James's study for a conversation that only two men could have on such an occasion. The two men entered the paneled room, both anticipating a much welcomed discourse. Dr. Terrell moved comfortably across the room. His gait mirrored the exuberance he felt at the prospect of his youngest daughter marrying what appeared to him to be a gentleman of quality, and good character. A father's dream come true. As James turned and gestured for Keino to sit in one of the handsome, oxblood colored leather recliners stationed in front of his well-used antique desk, he started speaking. His words were accentuated by the broad approving smile that he wore. "Keino, it goes without saying that I am very pleased with the idea of your marriage to Amara. Her mother and I have had our prayers answered this day." James continued speaking in calm, low tones as he took a seat opposite Keino in a matching recliner. He crossed his long legs and with a distant smile on his face, looking pointedly at Keino, he began to share what for him, James Terrell, were the most important things Keino needed to know about his daughter, and Keino's future wife. Keino moved forward slightly in his chair, clearly receptive to all of the wisdom that his future father-in-law had to impart.

"All of my daughters are special to me. Each one is her own person, and has her own unique way of facing the world. Amara, being the last to be born, is in many ways an interesting mixture of the three sisters before her. She can be as decisive as Adana, as mystical as Afiya, and as flamboyant as Cassandra. Yet there is the special piece which makes her Amara. She is a compassionate soul who wants to see the world free from pain and hunger. She loves deeply, and so, son, if she has given you her heart, it will always be yours to keep. Cherish that gift. You won't find anyone more loyal. Love her, son, and always treat her as the precious jewel that she is."

Keino's eyes brimmed with emotion as he drank in the tenderness with which his future father-in-law spoke about his wife-to-be. He spoke with equal intensity. "Dr. Terrell, I can promise you that I will love and cherish your daughter for the rest of my life. She will always have whatever she wants, if it is within my power to obtain it. The depth of my adoration for her can neither be explained, nor measured, and will not change even with my death."

When Keino finished speaking, James unfolded his long limbs and rose from his chair. When Keino followed his lead and stood, James grabbed him in a forceful bear hug, which Keino returned. James spoke in a voice laden with emotion. "Welcome to the family, son, and I want plenty of grandchildren."

In that moment they shared rich raucous laughter which truly cemented their bond.

Chapter 30

The weeks leading up to the wedding were a whirlwind of plans for the festivities which were to unite the Mazrui and Terrell families. Keino and Amara stole moments to be together while they both worked furiously to tie up loose ends in their businesses, and in their personal lives, before the wedding. Keino had determined that since the first three years of their marriage would be spent living on two continents, their honeymoon was scheduled to be one month, long enough to give them time to settle into one another, and to set up their living accommodations in both Nairobi and Virginia. Amara concurred that indeed they had much to put in place before, and after, the wedding.

Although the wedding was to be a private affair—just family and close friends—and though her mother and sisters were going to be a tremendous help, Amara knew she needed professional assistance, and so she enlisted the aid of a college friend who had become an internationally sought after events planner and wedding coordinator to be the point person. Amara had prevailed upon her old friend to fit her into her busy calendar. Camille Evanti, premier wedding planner, was flamboyant, driven, extremely well organized with impeccable taste, and a global world view. Camille was just the person Amara needed to pull together this extraordinary wedding.

The festivities would combine continental African traditions with African American ones, and last an extended period of three days, mimicking what in Africa could easily have been a seven day affair.

The week of the wedding, the Mazrui family flew to Virginia in the family jets, to begin the rounds of celebrations which would culminate in Keino and Amara's nuptials. At a private Virginia airstrip, Keino welcomed his parents, his brothers, their wives, and children, his Aunt Amara, the woman for whom his future wife was named, and her husband his uncle, Tafari Sellassie. General Sellassie, a retired military man, now served his country, Ethiopia, as an ambassador.

His marriage to Amara Sellassie had produced one son. They named him Ras Makail Sellassie. He was to have accompanied them on this trip but he had been delayed by his multiple business enterprises. From the moment of his birth Ras had never led a predictable life. His adventurous, rebellious spirit had made him the bane of his father's existence, and the love of his mother's life. As Keino welcomed his family, the anticipation of the merriment to come spilled over into each greeting. The Mazrui family felt and demonstrated a tremendous amount of love and affection for one another.

After the warm greetings, Keino's family was

shuttled to waiting limousines and driven to the city's most exclusive hotel, the Ambassador Arms, where a number of suites had been reserved on private floors which were only accessible to the Mazruis or their invited guests.

The Terrell household, like that of the Mazruis, was buzzing with excitement. Amara, Camille the wedding coordinator, and Amara's mother and sisters had designed a magnificent celebration which would honor the love that Keino and Amara shared, while also honoring the best of the grand traditions from both their ancestral cultures. Tonight was the first event. In Keino's home the two families would meet for the first time as a whole, and in grand continental African tradition with an African American twist, begin the round of events that would remain in the collective memories of both families for years to come.

Amara and her sisters were in their parents' home preparing for the evening's ceremony. The smiles and laughter were infectious. They were all so very happy for Amara, and Amara was as excited and as nervous as a child at Christmas awaiting Santa's arrival. Her sisters had finished dressing and had left her alone to put the finishing touches to her hair. As she put the last strands in place she heard a knock on the door of the bedroom she occupied. She responded to the rap on the door with a lighthearted, "Come in!"

The door opened and there stood her mother. Ana Terrell, upon seeing her daughter, could not hold back her joyous tears. Seeing the tears, Amara walked toward her mother saying gently, "Please, Mother, don't cry. I know they are happy tears but if you cry then I'll start. Please, Mom, don't cry."

As Amara softly touched her mother's cheeks to

dry her tears, Ana Terrell sniffed back flowing
tears and took a deep breath and cleared her
throat in order to allow herself to speak. "You are
right, my darling, this is not the time for tears. I
came in here to tell you how happy your father
and I are. We are so pleased with your choice and
we wish you a long and happy married life. We
know that with Keino you will find the kind of
peace and happiness your father and I have shared
over the years." Ana Terrell embraced her youngest
daughter, hoping that she could feel the love, the
joy, and the pride that was in her heart.

The first event was hosted by Keino at his home.
It was a ceremony designed to unite the two families. The limousines arrived bringing the members
of both families. When they entered Keino's property they were greeted by multiple trees festooned
with tiny crystal lights. The trees formed a ring
around the perimeter of the mansion, emitting a
blaze of white light. It was indeed a welcoming
sight. As the families left the parked limos and entered the foyer of the home, they were struck by a
transformation of space they could not possibly
have imagined. For this gathering the wedding
coordinator had transfigured Keino's expansive
living and dining rooms into a fantasy pavilion
draped in hundreds of yards of ecru and bronze
colored tulle from ceiling to floor. Hundreds of
candles and dim lighting set a romantic mood and
a wide array of enormous glass bowls strategically
placed around the room filled with floating gardenias added a pleasantly sweet fragrance to the air.
The feeling in the room was one of gaiety and elegance with a hint of mystery. Bronze colored, silk-
upholstered Parsons chairs were placed in a circle
in the middle of the large living room to accom-

modate all of the members of both families. When Amara walked through the door she could not have been more pleased. She and her friend Camille had agonized for hours over the design, wanting it to be reminiscent of African royalty of old, yet capturing also the glamour and beauty of contemporary times. As Keino walked slowly towards her, with one side of his mouth lifted in an equally slow smile, Amara could see that he was also pleased. The closer he came to her the more fragrant the air around him became. They shared a smile as he slipped his arm around her slender waist and murmured seductively, "You have outdone yourself. Thank you, my love. My parents will be forever grateful for your attempt to incorporate our traditions. This is just one of the many reasons why you were meant to be my wife."

Amara leaned contentedly into Keino's arms and said, "I'm glad you're pleased. It was a labor of love."

They then walked farther into the room in order to greet their guests together, and to begin the festivities. Keino and Amara took seats in the center of the circle facing each other, while the two families sat facing one another, on either side of the circle. Judge Mazuri stepped into the circle with an air of natural assurance and began to speak. His deep-timbered voice was filled with barely checked emotion as he began. "Welcome, everyone, to this ceremony that will unite the Mazuri and Terrell families. Traditionally at this point I would speak of the ceremonial history of the couple's proposal and engagement." He paused, and with a knowing smile and a glance first at Keino and then Amara, he continued. "All we know is that Keino Mazrui, our firstborn son, and Ms. Amara Terrell want to be husband and wife. The history of how they came to that conclusion will be one we will allow them to share with us when they choose as time goes by."

The onlookers smiled, knowing clearly that they would probably never be privy to the details of the passionate romance which had engulfed the two who sat in the center of the circle. Judge Mazrui continued. "However they came to be, Keino's mother Adina and I are delighted. We have never seen our son as smitten as he is by this wonderful young woman. We offer our thanks and our gratitude to you, Ana and James Terrell, for the magnificent upbringing of your daughter. She is a young woman of poise, grace, and intelligence and none of those characteristics outstrip her beauty."

With the conclusion of Judge Mazrui's statements the room went up in joyful shouts of agreement from the Mazrui brothers. Keino and Amara were sitting knee to knee, holding hands and laughing loudly like others in the room at the raucous display from Keino's brothers.

Calming the laughter Keino's mother, Adina, stood. With the remnants of a smile still on her face she said, "My dear Amara, as my husband has said, we are so very pleased to welcome you into our family. From the moment we met you and uncovered the origin of your name you had a special place in our hearts. My sister is here, as you know, and the two of us have presentations to make to welcome you into our family."

Keino's aunt stood and came forward. A taller, slightly older version of her sister, she walked over to Amara. Amara stood and they embraced. Keino's aunt, while dabbing at her misty eyes said, "Time has a way of bringing us such joy. When I discovered your existence it did indeed bring me joy.

Your mother and I shared such good times as young women, and I watched her love affair with your father blossom, and because of that Adina and I would like to give to you a piece of our mother's jewelry. It has much significance for us. It was the piece that father gave to our mother on the day that I was born."

Keino's Aunt Amara handed Amara Terrell a navy blue velvet case which Amara opened. Tears sprang to her eyes as she relished the beauty, and the sentiment, of the ornately carved platinum band encrusted with sapphire and diamond settings. She hugged Keino's Aunt Amara, and thanked her profusely. Keino's mother interjected, "Hold on, my darling, we are not finished. These next pieces have been in my husband's family for many years. They were saved by Keino's grandfather who is now deceased, for Keino to give to his bride. They officially bond you to the Mazuri family heritage."

Adina Mazrui handed two boxes to Keino. One contained the ring Amara would wear as Keino's bride. It was an elegantly cut marquise stone set on a platinum band. The second box contained an exquisite diamond necklace. Keino rose from his chair, took the ring from the box, and staring longingly and lovingly into Amara's teary eyes slipped the ring onto her finger. He knew the fit would be perfect because she was perfectly fashioned for him. The room went up in applause as Keino and Amara's embrace led to a soulful kiss.

James Terrell's time had come to speak and he was overwhelmed by the show of love and affection displayed towards his daughter. He stepped forward with his hands clasped as if in prayer. His long frame moved toward his daughter. He took her hand and spoke. "Mazrui family, my wife and I give our blessings for the marriage of Keino and Amara. Keino is a man among men. He has our daughter's heart and we are clear that he will cherish her for the rest of his life."

Standing between her father and her future husband, Amara looked around the room and felt a deep sense of peace and satisfaction. She felt so much joy and contentment. A warm glow eased over her. She gathered her thoughts and began to speak in quiet smooth tones. "I am overwhelmed by the love, kindness, and acceptance shown me tonight. I will forever cherish the memories of this ceremony. I love you all, and I am looking forward to being a Mazrui."

Keino stepped forward and with his perfect cadence and rich deep tones, thanked his parents, his aunt, the Terrells and his wife-to-be and began the traditional pouring of the libation. "Before the pouring of the libation, we ask for the blessings of God upon this marriage. May we live with ease and love. May we be blessed with healthy children, and now, for the libation."

A large, round bronze pot was placed in the middle of the circle. Waiters appeared seemingly from nowhere and provided everyone with a flute of champagne. A prayer was said and then each person in turn beginning with Judge Mazrui called out the name of an ancestor who had passed on. A sip was then taken from the champagne, and then a drop was poured in the bronze container. This part of the ceremony was solemn and an air of sacredness permeated the group. Emotions ran deep as the names of loved ones were called. As the last person in the circle brought forth the name of an ancestor, glasses were raised and Judge

Mazrui once again toasted Keino and Amara and the ceremony was completed.

After the ceremony the members of the two families were scattered about, enjoying newfound friendships and consuming delectable food and drink. Keino looked around the room for Amara. He found her engrossed in conversation with two of his brothers' wives. He stopped a few feet away from the group and looked on with awe and admiration at the beautiful picture Amara presented while standing there talking to her soon to be sisters-in-law. Her hands were gesturing and punctuating her speech, a habit of hers he found endearing. Her eyes were flashing, and her smile was brilliant. He loved this woman more than he could have imagined loving anyone. He had not known that such love was possible for him. In that moment he thanked all of the Divine forces for putting Amara in his path. As he continued standing and looking in the direction in which Amara stood, she felt his presence, looked up at him, smiled, excused herself from the group and began walking towards him. He stood legs apart, arms folded across his chest, and waited the brief moment it took for Amara to glide into his arms. As she entered the sphere in which he stood, he opened his arms and enfolded her in them. Her softness was intoxicating. His strength was for her like nectar. As they stood center to center he whispered lovingly in her ear, "I've missed you so. Waiting to have you forever in my life and in my bed is pure torture." With a straight face, and lust in his eyes, he spoke in a commanding tone. "Let's run away tonight." His sentence ended with a feathery breath that lingered as a kiss on the lobe of her ear.

"Keino, my love, we can wait a few more days and I promise I will be all yours." Amara teasingly tickled Keino's chin with her index finger and continued speaking softly to him, smiling while saying, "You're a big man, my sweet, surely you can let me go for just a few days longer."

Amara could feel the sexual tension and intense heat in Keino's response. He brought her closer, and while stroking both of her arms simultaneously whispered once again in her ear. "At this moment I want you more than life, but I will wait, and you will pay for my waiting. Now, let's go join our guests."

Amara was stunned, and stood trance-like for a moment. When she collected herself she smiled, took a deep breath and said to herself *I can't wait.*

The days that followed were filled with activities that involved either everyone in both families or segments of the two families.

The Mazrui wives and Amara's mother and sisters hosted a bridal shower. The stated objective of the shower was to find a gift for Amara that would bring pleasure to Keino. The gifts ran the gamut from beautiful lingerie and one-of-a-kind bath salts to his and hers masseuses, and a weekend in Paris flown in on the Concorde. The bridal shower provided the opportunity for the women to really get to know one another and to renew old acquaintances. Amara's mother and Keino's aunt were particularly delighted to reconnect and vowed never to lose touch again. The Mazrui men, James Terrell, and Tafari Sellassie, Keino's uncle, spent the day golfing and ribbing Keino about the perils of being a husband. The eighteen holes of golf and the early supper that followed provided the men with a much needed and very satisfying bonding experience. They all left the day's events knowing that they had made lifelong connections.

Keino, in his customary impatient style, continued to telephone Amara at least twice a day impressing upon her his need for her and his impatience with the movement of time. Amara continued to laugh and to reassure him that time really was moving, and that soon they would be husband and wife, and that she would forever be there to rein in his impatient spirit.

Amara was stretched out across her bed, her nude body covered with a lightweight chenille throw. She was preparing for a much needed nap when her phone rang. She really needed a nap. The round of events with the two families had been wonderfully exhilarating but equally tiring. The telephone rang again. Her instincts told her not to ignore the ring because if her future husband happened to be on the other end, he would not rest until he heard her voice. A lazy warmth poured over her as she simultaneously picked up the receiver and thought wistfully of her impatient lover. The moment she spoke her silken "Hello," she knew she had been correct to answer the call. Keino's voice was heavy with longing and need as he said, "Amara, I don't want to wait any longer. I need you, today, this instant. I need to feel all of you. I need to touch you with every fiber of my being. I need you. I need you to come to me."

Amara's entire body reacted violently to Keino's pleading. His uncompromising tones, the deep sensuality of his words set her on fire. It always amazed her that Keino could, with just his words, send her into pools of ecstasy. She hovered between mindless obedience and adhering to the expected decorum. She stilled her smoldering body, closed her eyes, took a deep breath and responded to Keino with faltering determination. "Keino, darling, please don't do this. Soon we can be together whenever, wherever we want. Please darling, just one more night. I want you as badly as you want me but I want us to get through this. The next time I make love to you it will be as your wife. As it is we have defied tradition. Let's keep something. I do love you so. You know I do."

Keino's tone cooled though his passion did not, as he responded, "Amara, you are the only woman for whom at a time like this I will push my desires aside and adhere to yours." His tone a bit lighter he said, "All right, my darling, I will leave you to your day. By the way, what are you doing?"

Amara stifled a laugh, knowing the scene she would paint in Keino's mind as she gingerly stated, "I am in my bedroom. I was preparing to take a much needed nap."

Keino's deep laughter burst through the phone wires as he said, "Here I am a drowning man and I am supposed to spend the rest of my day with a picture in my head of your honey colored, perfectly formed naked body. Amara, my darling, you are so cruel. You refuse me and leave me with a picture of your exquisite body which I cannot touch, roaming lazily through my mind. Please at least tell me you are not naked."

Amara, with a grin that stretched from one end of her face to the other said, "All right, my darling, I will tell you. I am not naked." Just as Keino was about to breathe a sigh of relief thinking he had been given a bit of a reprieve, Amara added, "But, my darling, I cannot lie. I am as naked as the day I was born." She quietly dropped the receiver into its cradle, snuggled under her soft comfortable throw, smiled and said aloud, "God, how I love that man." She closed her eyes and once again attempted to chase an elusive slumber.

Keino swore, shook his head from side to side, laughed at the quick-witted Amara and headed off to take a cold shower, a process with which he had become all too familiar.

The evening of the final gathering of the two families before the wedding was designed to be fun for all, and included a host of close personal friends. After a quick rehearsal run-through at Keino's private club, which had been chosen as the site of the wedding ceremony, the families, and additional invited guests, were hosted aboard a one hundred sixty foot chartered yacht. The dinner was an elegant array of smoked salmon, smoked trout, lobster salads, beef Wellington, sliced tomatoes with green basil sauce, summer potato salad with walnut dressing and an assortment of fruits, cheeses, and French desserts. Champagne flowed endlessly to quench any thirst. Entertainment was provided by Astair, an Ethiopian songstress whose melodic tones brought out the romantic in everyone aboard. Her soft engaging style blended magically with the cool evening breezes. A Kenyan dance troupe and a jazz saxophonist rounded out the evening. As the saxophonist played, Keino took every opportunity to dance with Amara and hold her in his arms. He told her many times during the evening that she would pay dearly for her telephone humor. Each time he mentioned the conversation, Amara was unable to stop laughing. Onlookers assumed, and rightfully so, that the soon-to-be marrieds were sharing a private joke. Much to the surprise and delight of Amara and Keino, Bradford Donald and Veronica Strong had been inseparable the entire evening.

The morning of her wedding, Amara awoke, looked around her room, and knew that her life would after this day, never be the same. She lifted herself from her bed and reached into the chair beside her and pulled a multicolored caftan over her head. She slipped into a pair of very comfortable mules and made her way into her bathroom to wash her face and brush her teeth, after which she headed downstairs to her kitchen. She was about to put on a pot for tea and go back upstairs to bathe and prepare for her day when her doorbell rang. A bit puzzled as to who could be calling so early in the morning she answered her door and was greeted by a courier. He was a pleasant-looking, tall, slender young man of Middle Eastern decent.

"Good morning. I have a package for Ms. Amara Terrell."

"Well, good morning to you, too," Amara replied with as much cheer as she felt. "I am Amara Terrell."

The young man moved a little closer and said, smiling, "Would you sign here please and I'll gladly give you this package."

Amara signed, took the package, thanked the courier, and hurried inside to satisfy her curiosity. She walked back into the kitchen, sat down at the counter and began to open the package. The signature wrapping let her know that the gift had come from Tiffany's, and the moment she saw the note attached she knew from whom it had come. Keino's bold scrawl was unmistakable. He wrote:

My darling Amara,

In just a few hours you will be my wife, my bride. I will adore you until we both cease to live, and even then the remnants of my passion for you will be flickering throughout the universe. These two tokens were chosen as my gifts to you on our wedding day. Wear them, if you will, in honor of our love.

Ever yours,
Keino

Amara opened the box and found the most beautiful pearl and diamond necklace with matching teardrop earrings she had ever seen. The beauty of Keino's words and the beauty of the jewels left her eyes moist and her heart full. Just as she dried her eyes her telephone rang. She answered to find all of her sisters on the line at the same time. Adana, no doubt, allowing her office habits to spill over into her family life, Amara thought with a gleam in her eye.

"Well this is great! I get to talk to all of my sisters on the telephone at once. Adana this had to be your idea."

"Guilty," was Adana's response.

"I thought it would be a great way for all of us to check up on you, see how you're holding up. Any second thoughts?"

Amara's quick retort was, "My second and third thoughts are why didn't this man show up in my life sooner and will five-thirty P.M. hurry up so that I can become his wife. He just sent me the most beautiful necklace and earrings today. He is so thoughtful and so good to me. I just love him so."

"All right now!" was Cassandra response. She continued in her own flamboyant style. "Miss Thang

you know you have the right idea. Amara you have
made the right decision, sweetie, and you know we
wish you all the best."

Afiya chimed in with a voice shrouded in mystery and laced with humor. "Amara, you know I
consulted the stars, the I Ching, the tarot and the
cartouche, and every spirit in the universe is on
your side."

With that the sisters erupted in gales of laughter. Adana, again the organizer, said, as soon as she
could control her own laughter, "Okay, enough,
enough, we will meet you in three hours for the
hair-makeup-dress ritual. Since we are your brides-
maids we must be fine. See you, sweetie."

They all rang off, and Amara shook her head
while still laughing. She decided against making
water for tea and headed back upstairs to begin
her morning ablutions with visions of Keino dancing in her head.

Keino was pacing like a panther. His brothers,
who had arrived for moral support, and to be his
groomsmen, sat watching him until Kaleb said,
"Brother, is it your intention to wear a hole in the
carpet, or are you really on a journey with all of
this walking. Where are you going?"

A crooked smile settled on Keino's face and he
stood still, looked at his brothers, and said, "I
guess I *am* pacing. I am anxious to be married; I
want the formalities to be over, I want my wife."

Aman stretched his long legs in front of him as
he sat on a comfortable seat. He nodded his head
affirmatively while saying, "We understand, big
brother, we've all been there. Calm down, the time
will soon pass."

Kamau, almost as nervous as Keino, jumped to his feet, walked to Keino, and placed a strong protective hand on an equally solid shoulder and said, "I think it is time for me to go and get our father; his calming influence is definitely needed now."

Kaleb, the jokester said, "Yes, you are right, Kamau, we would not want our brother to self-destruct."

They all shared the humor of Kaleb's remarks.

The wedding was an elegant, intimate affair. The only guests were the two families and their closest friends. The guest list did not exceed one hundred. Keino's private club, which had been retained for the ceremony and the reception, was exquisitely decorated. It was an evening affair lit by shimmering candles and low romantic lights. Cascades of lilies, beautifully scented gardenias, and stephanotis filled the room. Fine china held by golden chargers graced each place setting, announced by calligraphied place cards. Guests were served an array of canapés and entrees from America, Kenya, and Ethiopia. Imported champagne, chilled and flowing, graced every toast.

Amara was for Keino a vision of angelic beauty in a simply cut ecru and ivory, floor-length, off-the-shoulder gown. Her hair was swept up, enhanced by strategically placed baby's breath. Keino's gifts of necklace and matching pearl earrings graced her ears and neck.

Keino was Amara's knight in shining armor dressed in black formal wear with pearl buttons on his ivory colored collarless shirt and pearl cuff links in his sleeves. The ceremony was performed by both Amara's family minister and Keino's mother's brother Menilek, an Ethiopian Coptic priest. The vows were said in a ritual imitating ancient African tradition. Keino, Amara and the officiates stood in the middle of a circle formed by Garsen and Adina Mazrui and their children, and James and Ana Terrell and their children, symbolizing the community into which Amara and Keino were marrying. The room stilled as Keino and Amara recited their vows. The essence of their love hovered in the air like a gentle mist on an early winter morning. The beauty of the ceremony could only be matched by the gaiety of the reception. A jazz orchestra provided sounds old and new that thrilled the guests. Keino and Amara danced and laughed and generally enjoyed the festivities, going from table to table thanking their guests and receiving loving embraces and well wishes from everyone.

Keino's Aunt Amara and Ana Terrell were so happy to see one another again, they reverted to being old college chums vowing to always stay in touch.

While the guests chattered and reveled in the celebration, Ras Sellassie sat at a table with his parents. He surveyed the reception room with all of its merrymaking, with a distance that might have been perceived as coldness if one did not know him. He had arrived just in time to hear the vows said and to congratulate his cousin and his new bride. He loved Keino, and since they had been reared like brothers they were closer than most cousins. Ras nevertheless, had his mind on business and in spite of his loyalty to Keino, he was just about to make his exit as quickly and as unobtrusively as he had made his entrance when his eyes honed in like a beam of light on the table where

Amara's sisters sat. There she was, a beauty he knew he had to touch. As the orchestra began a slow melodic tune, he excused himself from the table where he sat, and began slow pondered steps toward Adana, Cassandra, and Afiya.

As the music played and Amara's sisters chatted about Amara and Keino and the life they would live, and the beautiful babies they would produce, Cassandra saw her sisters freeze as if in suspended animation, and at the same time she felt a touch on her bare back. Then she heard a composed velvet murmur float across her ears.

"Excuse me, may I have this dance?"

As she turned she could see why her sisters had frozen. There he stood, six feet three inches tall, with an athletic build, toffee colored skin with hair like the feathers of a raven. It was cut short so that it fell in front with a hint of a wave. His face was angular, his cheekbones high, his mouth very full and his eyes intense. He stepped back with a smoothness that was ethereal, and extended his hand. Cassandra placed her hand in his, lifted herself from the chair, and he guided her into his arms as though she belonged there. As they glided across the floor to the strains of the mellow music, the devastatingly handsome man with the heart wrenching appeal spoke again. "Allow me to introduce myself. I am Ras Sellassie, Keino's cousin. Our mothers are sisters. I almost missed the festivities but no amount of business could keep me from watching my cousin say his vows, and I must say, spotting you from across the room was an added bonus."

Cassandra had trouble finding her voice. His speech, clipped and sure, sent waves of excitement

through her. She answered with as much composure as she could muster. "My name is Cassandra
Terrell. I am the bride's sister."

A jumble of confused emotions surged through
her as Ras stated, "Ah yes, I can see that the loveliness is duplicated."

The introductions finished, they continued to
sway with the music, each lost in intriguing thoughts
of the other. Ras was clear that he was going to
make it his business to get to Keino, and find out
more about this very desirable woman.

As Afiya and Adana watched their sister dance
with the mystery man, Afiya leaned over to Adana
and whispered, looking in the direction of her
dancing sister, "If I could consult my magic shells,
I'd bet they would tell me that Cassandra is in for
the ride of her life."

Adana tilted her head and with a wistful smile
said, "Afiya, this time I have to agree with you."

With that observation the two of them fell back
into the easy banter with which they were so accustomed.

At the reception's end, Keino and Amara were
whisked away for a honeymoon back to Curacao
where their love had first been sealed. As they
were being ushered away they both knew that what
had started as a foreign affair would bring them
both a lifetime of pleasure. True to his word,
Keino made Amara pay dearly for making him
wait, and she loved every minute spent paying with
passion-filled kisses, and lovemaking designed to
satiate a hunger only the two of them possessed.